YOU ARE AMONG MONSTERS

YOU ARE AMONG MONSTERS

JON R. FLIEGER

Copyright © 2017 Jon R. Flieger

All rights reserved

Palimpsest Press
1171 Eastlawn Ave.
Windsor, Ontario. N8S 3J1
www.palimpsestpress.ca

Book and cover design by Kate Hargreaves (CorusKate Design)
Edited by Aimée Dunn
Copy edited by Ginger Pharand

Palimpsest Press would like to thank the Canada Council for the Arts, and the Ontario Arts Council for their support of our publishing program. We also acknowledge the assistance of the Government of Ontario through the Ontario Book Publishing Tax Credit.

Library and Archives Canada Cataloguing in Publication

Flieger, Jon R., 1983-, author
You are am[o]ng monsters / Jon R. Flieger.

The "o" in the word among appears as a skull.

Issued in print and electronic formats.

ISBN 978-1-926794-57-0 (softcover).--
ISBN 978-1-926794-58-7 (PDF)

I. Title.

PS8611.L57Y68 2017   C813'.6
C2017-902872-3   C2017-902873-1

PRINTED AND BOUND IN CANADA

~~There is a story in there, somewhere~~

PART 1
TRANSFER

What wish is enacted, what desire is gratified, by the fantasy that real events are properly represented when they can be shown to display the formal coherency of a story?
—HAYDEN WHITE

IAN

We call it a transfer. Getting the terms right is a big part of the job. It's important to use the terms, to distance yourself. It's a dead guy in the back of a van, really, but the words can be something else. Hauling dead bodies around is another big part. I pick up a transfer from an accident site, not a dead guy. Not a guy anymore, not even a corpse. I don't say corpse, or cadaver, body. It's upsetting to the family if they are on hand, so I call it a transfer. The funeral home calls it remains if they have to call it anything. Euphemisms are one of the primary services the death industry offers. Kindness and lies in language. Also, we deal with your dead. I say "we" when I have to speak to the bereaved. I say bereaved and not mourners. Or dead guy's relatives. I say "we" because people are comforted by the concept that I am part of something larger and organized and that it's not simply me and my partner loading their dead into the back of a van and taking them away. I say very little. I collect what needs collecting and I disappear. I don't work for a hospital. I drive a van, not an ambulance. Not a hearse. If I'm there it's because it was a No Chance. The paramedics, the police, the rescue workers are already gone or they didn't bother. If you get your head cut off by farm equipment on the outskirts of a small town they don't send the ambulance out, the tires squealing, the sirens blaring. Because then what? Yup. Motherfucker's head sure is off.

Yup.

They don't wake the doctor up for that one.

No Chance accidents. The elderly who pass quietly in their rest homes. The people not seen for a while whose neighbours complain about a stink wafting through the apartment complex. If the body isn't prepared for burial, they don't send a hearse. If the body cannot be saved, they don't send an ambulance. They send two guys in a van. I wear black but no tie and shake as few hands as possible. Get in and out as quickly as I can unless the other guy riding with me is a funeral director. They always want to hang around all day pumping the family for information and trying to sell. Shaking hands and offering condolences but smiling. I make sure I get signatures on the proper forms because I don't want to have to go back. I'm not the Grim Reaper, no matter how many times that furious bitch at the Naglfar Family Rest Home curses me out. I just take the body. And I call it a transfer.

I'm saying "it" now but really I try not to do that either. People get upset. "It" used to be a he. A him. A father. Whatever. The act is a transfer and the remains themselves are a transfer. It is a noun and a verb and a word that avoids other words. It is versatile. It is useful to me. I try not to use the name of the deceased. One: because it can be upsetting, and two: because I forget the names the minute after I read them. I work for a transfer service. Becky calls me the boatman. Says I ferry the souls across the river but she's wrong. She was a grad student back east and as a consequence she reads too much. And reads too much into everything. Not everything has to mean something. Why does anyone do anything? I just transfer.

The kid sitting next to me is named Neal. Or Ned. Something. This is the first transfer he's been on. This is training. All he has to do today is help me lift but he's nervous.

"Do you get used to it?" he asks.

Get used to what?

"Bodies. Dead bodies. That. That gets easier. Right?"

Call them transfers. Don't talk to anyone on site if you can help it. You have gloves?

"Yeah I have my gloves."

Check. Make sure.

"They're right here."

Always make sure you have your gloves. Seriously.

"Okay."

Don't snap your gloves if you can help it. It weirds the family out.

"Jesus, will there be family there?"

Probably not at this one.

I'll teach him more later. I'll also make him fill out the paperwork because I hate doing it.

"I'm kind of freaking out a little."

You're supposed to. Don't worry.

But I don't know if he is supposed to. He might not last. We have pretty high turnover which is why this kid is riding next to me and nervously popping his knuckles every thirty seconds. Gerry quit. Dan before him. Lots more whose names I don't remember. I didn't freak out on my first transfer. I disappointed myself when—

But then we see the smoke.

"Jesus Christ."

Yup.

"Is that us? That can't be us, right? I thought we had to go way out."

That's us. You see the smoke a long way on the prairie.

"Oh."

He's from Toronto. Every time I need him to shut up I'll remind him this isn't Toronto. That is shitty of me but fuck it. He talks a lot. The less you talk on this job, the less you think about the work itself, the better. That's cliché maybe but I touch dead people every day of my life. I know what they do at the funeral home with the soft skulls of infants so that they can be preserved for a viewing without collapsing. That sometimes a pacemaker gets forgotten and has to be fished out of a viscera bag so that it doesn't explode in the cremation retort. When a woman promised her mother she would tickle her feet at the funeral to make sure she was really dead I had to explain to her in soft words that she didn't want to do that. To not say that, even if the withered corpse was somehow not dead when it arrived on my table, after I stabbed a metal spike into its thorax and aspired the viscera from her body, it was well and thoroughly dead now. Instead, I told her that mom was in our care and it was our job to make sure she didn't have anything to worry about. A soft joke about the socks I put on her for the funeral being pretty itchy. She's at rest now; she's in our care. Cliché is important. It's another euphemism we offer. This kind of specificity does not need to be discussed. The first reaction is always to talk. Offer condolences if the family is there. Commiserate with the other transfer agent or the cops or paramedics or whatever at an accident. But the impulse is wrong. Language is a failing here, it makes you deal with—

And with—

"Jesus that's a lot of smoke."

Yeah.

These ones—these messes at the sides of highways—in a way they're easier. Don't have to get signatures from rest home administration or permission from landlords to enter. The police or fire or whoever is at the scene will sign so they can go home and we'll go to work. This is a job that someone has to do. I'm someone. Neal or Ned might be, we'll see. As we approach the smoke billow I slow the van. Blips of light pulse against the underplume of smoke. Cops or fire on site already. That's good. But too far to the north. Ah fuck.

Ah fuck.

"What?" the kid asks, suddenly panicked.

The smoke is coming from the field. The truck must have thrown the transfer's car. We're gonna have to walk in.

I don't think we have to get permission from the farmer if the cops are already on scene. I could call my boss for procedure on this or I could just get the transfer out and claim ignorance later if I have to. That one gets me to lunch faster.

"There are crows up there." Neal or Ned watches them circle high and lazy, avoiding the thickest parts of the smoke.

There is little wind today. Birds and a pillar of ashy dark smoke hang in the air.

Yeah. There are always birds on the outdoors ones.

"Oh Jesus it smells like cooking."

Don't. Just turn off. Try not to think about it. And if the birds have been at it, try not to look at the face.

"What?"

They take the eyes first.

"Fuck."

The kid probably won't last long enough for me to learn his name. I pull the van to a stop. Fire and cops have already done what little they were going to do. I see a familiar cop. Nod to him as I kill the van's engine and grab my clipboard. The cop nods back and stretches his neck. Looks at his watch. With us on scene and everything contained, they can leave once they get me to sign off. A No Chance.

The story goes something like this: an eighteen-bajillion-ton truck hauling two trailers and doing about thirty over the limit comes smashing down the Crowsnest and hits the transfer's little Hyundai. The transfer must have been shooting through on one of the intersecting county roads but it's impossible to tell where the actual impact happened. There are pieces and wreckage flung everywhere. Rubber on the road but it's unlikely the trucker reacted fast enough to hit the air brakes at that speed. That much mass and velocity will throw debris a quarter mile into the field. The transfer and his Hyundai fireballed. Fire on scene got most of it out, but parts are still smouldering. As I wade into the field stung and flayed by whiptails of wheat I see the rear-view mirror sitting on the ground between rows of crop, detached and unbroken. Just there. The truck has barely any damage. Too heavy, too fast. The juggernaut sits, still ticking and abandoned as the unhurt driver is taken into custody. Called the accident in himself. Could have just driven away. Nice guy. Except for his speeding having killed a man, I guess. But still. Me and the kid go to work. The car was made of steel and the impact reduced it to pieces. The transfer was not made of steel. I feel bad for the kid. This is not a good first transfer. But I guess there isn't a good first transfer. This isn't easy, anyway. In the field like this we can't get the stretcher in, just bags. And since the transfer isn't in one piece it's… Well, it's awkward and heavy. Lumpy black shopping bags. The kid vomits as loudly as he can. I keep looking around. When the birds stay you know you missed pieces. Eventually I give up. Birds settle and perch on pieces of twisted wreckage. They watch me. Fuck. I hate the birds. The kid retches again.

You okay, man?
"Fuck you. Fuck you, I quit."
Yeah.

Poor kid. On the way back to town he calls me a monster and a ghoul and then a monster again and just kind of cycles in his little breakdown. The smell in the van doesn't help him.

He pukes in his lap and makes no move to clean himself up, just sits in it and stares out the window. I hit play again on the Pixies CD I've left in the van for the past year. The first stop light we hit in the town he gets out. Slams the door. Just stalks off covered in his own sick. There is a good sandwich place in this block but maybe I'll get back first. My keychain clicks against the steering column as I wait for the light to turn green. The Pixies scratch out of the speakers at me. Without someone to provide euphemism for, I know the transfer for what he is as he rides behind me. Heaviness of char and bone and meat.

I open the front door and kick my shoes off. I hear Becky in the kitchen.

Hey.

"Oh, hey," she calls. I hear the fridge open. Close. "You're home early. Will you be here for dinner?"

Yeah.

I straighten my shoes on the stupid dogface-shaped shoe mat.

I mean unless someone dies.

"Don't say it like that."

Okay. Sorry.

"Hard day?"

I walk to the archway that separates the kitchen from the front hallway. Is that a foyer? I don't know what a foyer is. It sounds too nice to be part of our shitty little house, though. I take my time. Don't need to be in the kitchen at the same time. Would like to not be. What did she say?

What did you say? Sorry.

"Did you have a hard day? You sound tired." She asks this like she's accusing me. *You* sound tired. Like I shouldn't. Or I'm imagining that, I don't know, fuck it. I'm tired. She's got the kitchen torn apart. Cleaning the fridge. Or something. She hates me when she does domestic anything. She'll refer to herself as a *hausfrau* and act like she gave fucking bone marrow all night. Her hair is in a red knot on top of her head, her glasses smudged with fingerprints. U of T sweatshirt. The kid called me a monster.

Not the greatest day, I guess. Messy.

"Oh, yuck. Don't tell me about it." Waits a moment. "It couldn't be much worse than *this* I guess." She laughs but it's a hollow, clacking sound. Yeah. Cleaning the kitchen is as bad as picking pieces of charred copse out of a field. You got me. Okay, maybe I'm just being shitty.

Do you want me to—

"No, no. It's fine. I'm nearly done now anyway." God she hates me. She stops for a moment, makes a face and "It wasn't. Well, it wasn't anyone we know was it?"

No. Wasn't local.

"Good."

Yeah.

"Well, not good."

No, I know what you mean.

I hang my jacket up, wash my hands, then wander back to the kitchen. Should probably go sit in the bedroom and lie low if she's on a cleaning spree but I'm stupid.

The new kid went out with me today. He quit.

"Nate? He quit already?" Nate. Right.

Yeah. Wasn't a good first day. Poor kid was sick.

"I'm surprised you're not sick more often." I shrug.

"I guess you've gotten used to it."

I guess.

"I'll make chicken for dinner, I think."

Fuck.

Okay. Yum.

Plain black dress shirt. Plain black slacks. Plain black socks. All Walmart issue. The shirt and pants ironed to a shine and the socks pilly from the washing machine. I don't need to look nice to pick up the transfers, just presentable and forgettable. Now that Becky is staying at home and doing more of the chores my clothes will last a little longer. She's better at laundry than I am, but I hate when she does it. I don't expect her to. I try to help. Generally it starts a fight.

"Well I may as well do *something*."

Okay but, like, you don't have to.

And then she'll take a book into the bedroom and read so angrily I can feel it from the other room. Or sink down into a chair and go catatonic in front of a DVD of cartoons played at top volume. She lost her job. She's not doing research anymore. She has no access to research materials here. I get that. But it's not my fault.

Okay well it's sort of my fault. She hates Alberta. She was happier in Toronto. She was happy in Detroit. She didn't even have a driver's licence until we moved here. She hasn't acclimated that well to living among people who have never seen a street-car. She likes to google how long it would take us to drive to a museum. A gallery. A restaurant that isn't a greasy spoon or a McDonald's. A city type of anything. She likes to tell me how many minutes. Hours. She moved here for me. So I could finish training as a funeral director and work as a transfer agent. She got a crappy temporary job at the drug store. She lost it. She does housework now that doesn't need to be done. And she does it *at* me.

I strip off my plain black shirt, plain black slacks, plain black socks and toss them in the hamper. I think better of it and take them back out. She did laundry yesterday. I didn't get any mess on me despite the scavenger hunt in the field and there's only a bit of dirt on my pants. I can wear everything again tomorrow. I fold the clothes and put them in my drawers of the dresser. Catch sight of myself in the mirror. In my boxers and getting a little fat. I'll be thirty-one next week. Becky said she's going to bake me a cake. I'm dreading it.

Fat old man. My hair is still thick, at least. I palm it away from my forehead. Check for recession in the hairline. Small mercies, my father's heredity has been denied. Or is hair supposed to be from the mother's side? Is that just an urban myth? I think grandpa had a full head of hair when he died but I don't remember. He usually wore a fishing cap. And he was an asshole. But I am definitely gaining weight. I flex in the mirror.

"Sexy," Becky says from the doorway. My entire body blushes above the dresser.

I'm. Uh.

"Do you want potatoes with dinner? Or rice?"

Um. Potatoes? Please.

"Kay."

I always choose potatoes given the opportunity. Probably why I'm getting fat. I pretend to be busy looking for my pajama pants in the dresser and mumble thank you.

"What for?"

For potato choice. For making dinner.

"I always do," she sighs. Or says. But maybe sighs.

Fucking stupid. I walk right into these things. For a moment I consider saying "and I always pay the rent" but even I'm not that stupid.

I love you.

She blinks.

"I love you too." And she goes back to the kitchen. I flex in the mirror again. You'd think I'd be in better shape from all the lifting. My reflection in the mirror looks back disappointed. For a monster, I'm looking kind of doughy. I make a mouth out of the flab around my belly button. The hair running down in a line into my boxer shorts looks like a little beard. I make the mouth say "Fuck you, Nate. Why don't you sit in your own puke like an animal some more? Call me a monster, you little shit?" and then I get bored. I put on a Batman t-shirt that Becky got me and some pajama pants. I sit on the bed and play with my phone, out of Becky's way until dinner is ready.

BECKY

Ian says he'll clean up after dinner. Why doesn't she go read or something? Just relax for a while. He thinks he is being kind but it sounds condescending to Becky. He feels guilty. Or she imagines he feels guilty. Or must, because Becky always does the cooking. Because she's always home. Which she hates. She doesn't want to guilt him into doing things but she also doesn't want to clean the dishes so she leaves him to it and goes into the TV room. She considers doing readings for her PhD application but decides she is too tired. She sinks into the saggy brown armchair and hunts for the TV and DVD remotes amongst the books and elastic-banded bags of potato chips on the end table. *The Jetsons* DVD is still in the player and she hits "PLAY ALL."

George Jetson works three hours a day. Three days a week. Jane doesn't work at all. In the future being a housewife is progress. Becky concedes that Jane does have that bitchy robot and all those machines. Becky likes the 1960s *Jetsons* better than the 1980s version. They talk more about rockets and less about super computers. Becky has an iPhone, but she has never owned a rocket. Maybe twenty years of fearing bombs changed rocket into a dirty word, she thinks. But *The Jetsons* should have been a comfort. Everyone is still alive and George doesn't speak Russian. Becky considers that they don't live on the ground in the future—they all live up on those floating platforms. Maybe the nuclear annihilation of the surface world is subtext in *The Jetsons* and Becky has been a bad reader. She muses. The world burnt to dust. Holocaust below and shining steel and glass rising into the clouds. Her eyes go glossy. She tries to remember if she's ever seen a non-white person on the show. Can't think of one.

"Gee-whiz," Elroy says on the screen as his future machines explode in a shower of not very futuristic looking cogs, springs, and gears.

"Gee-whiz," says Becky.

"Honey, can you turn that down a little?" Ian bellows from the kitchen.

"It's only on 20."

"Okay. Sorry. It's just kind of loud."

"Fine."

19, 18, 17, 18. The explosions and incidental music on-screen die down, so Becky waits a moment and then 19, 20.

"Thanks, honey."

"Mmm-hmm."

A few minutes later Ian brings Becky a can of Diet Coke. A beer for himself.

"Oh. Thanks." Astro scrambles to escape Elroy's machines. "We still have beer in the house?"

"Last one." He sits on the edge of the futon on the other side of the end table. "Sorry." Scans the table quickly but Becky has the remotes protected in her lap.

"What's this?" He gestures at the screen with his chin. "Scooby-Doo?"

"Jetsons."

"That isn't Scooby-Doo?"

"No. That's Astro. He has a futuristic space collar, see?"

"Oh, right."

"Scooby-Doo is brown."

"What's the name of that guy in Scooby-Doo?"

"Shaggy."

"No, not that one. The one who looks like a Hardy Boy. Like a boy scout."

"Oh, the blonde one? Fred."

"The kid who quit today kind of looked like that."

"Did he wear a little kerchief?"

"What?"

"Never mind."

They watch Astro fall victim to another of Elroy's machines on-screen. Robotic arms with big white gloves on the end snake out of a semi-futuristic looking Easy-Bake Oven and Astro is pulled along the floor towards it. The scene is vaguely horrifying.

"Ru-roh," Becky says.

"Astro. Futuristic space pet. They should have named the dog 'Laika,'" Ian laughs at his own joke.

"No, I think the subtext is that the Russians lost."

"What?"

"Never mind."

Getting never-minded twice seems to annoy Ian and he takes a fast swig of his beer. Becky regrets shutting him down but it's not really an apology moment. They let the air hang thick with domestic politics. There is another explosion scene and they both wince at how loud the TV is but neither says anything.

"I think I used to have an album called 'Laika Come Home,'" he says after a minute.

"That's so sad," she says, pretending interest to apologize for shutting down his earlier joke.

"Really? I never saw it as sad. I thought it was funny."

She raises an eyebrow but does not look at him.

They sit quietly for a few minutes and watch sprockets and springs fly. He doesn't really like cartoons; he's just putting in couple time. Peace restored, he takes his beer into the bedroom to watch YouTube videos on his laptop.

On-screen rockets fly. George zips off to work alone in his little flying car. Becky is 29 and unemployed. She lives in a small house in a small town in Alberta with a man who carries dead bodies for a living. She has a master's degree in history and wanted to be a teacher. Or a writer. Or something. When she reduces her thoughts and life to these small, simple facts, she pretends she is documenting herself, somehow. Preserving herself in history. Allowing bias. Acknowledging it. Resentment encasing it like amber. Restless, she paws through the books and papers next to her chair and gets out the scant materials she has assembled to apply to PhD work at the University of Bow River. Again. Her previous rejections are in the stack of materials to keep her honest. She holds them in her lap as she watches *The Jetsons* but can't quite seem to read them with the future unfolding before her in animated technicolor. The problem with history is that there is no future in it.

"Ian? Ian, listen to this."

"Huh."

"Read this part. Here." She pushes the book at him. Her fingernail stabbing at a spot on the page. "No wait. Start at this line."

"Ugh. I was just falling asleep." He lies next to her in their bed. He adopts the strangest positions. His one arm up above his head and propped parallel to the headboard. His other arm tucked between his knees.

"No just read this one part, it's about death and how people treat it, it'll interest you. Nigel Barley is the author."

"That name doesn't mean anything to me. Should it?"

"I don't know. Just read it."

"Read it to me."

"Fine. Hold on." She settles back, pokes him when he tries to roll over. "No, listen. Okay, here.

Having stripped death of its cosmological components, Western culture frequently views death as a social worker's problem that requires emotional counselling. Elsewhere it may be felt that the required training is rather in how to kill others magnificently.

When discussing this book, I found many people assuming that, as an anthropologist, I would conclude the West has got death all wrong and that the Bong-Bongo, or whoever, have got it properly sorted out. There was a belief that there must be a simple off-the-peg ritual we can bolt on to make death 'all right' and turn its sting into a kiss. But every view of death generates its own problem, one that often seems to have been deliberately set up in order to be insoluble, so the primary value of studying other views of death is, perhaps, to learn how little our own view is given by Nature. We could change if we wanted to—but we do have to want to. To counsel others on such matters requires great wisdom, humanity and judgement and these are not part of any recognized academic discipline."

"Isn't that great?" No answer. For a second she thinks he's fallen asleep and prepares to launch unholy vengeance upon him. But then he speaks.

"I guess. Kind of racist, isn't it? 'Bong-Bongo, or whoever'?"

"Not really. And that's not the point. Just like, how everyone deals with death and no matter what, maybe we haven't figured it out. And that stuff about the cruelty of the academy. I think it's great."

"I guess." He rolls over again and this time she lets him go un-poked. "People always want to 'deal' with death. Talk about it. But then they die anyway."

"It's not about that."

"I guess I didn't understand it, then." He curls into a surprisingly small ball for a tall man and then he's asleep. Becky reads for another half hour and then turns her light off and curls into the warmth he creates in the bed. Angles her body against his curved spine. His body temperature soars when he sleeps. They have not had sex in three months. He touches dead women more than he touches me, she thinks, and she's considered saying this to him but it seems too forceful. Too cliché for a situation that can't actually be common enough to be cliché. Too malicious despite the malice she feels. Too immature. And he'll just counter with her own lack of initiating, like the last time they fought. Fighting about sex. In rural Alberta. She is 29 and wants to write. She does not need him but she remembers wanting to need him. He is currently paying the rent and they can't afford to live like this much longer. She does need him. In a base survival sense. Love used to be the consideration. Now practicality. But only that? No, she thinks. No not yet. She presses her breasts around the notches of his spine. Curls her legs up next to his and feels the warmth of his body. He's gained a little weight, she thinks. Has she? She doesn't think so. The city. The Great Lakes. The things Becky left behind her. Ian does not want children. She doesn't either, but she feels it is worse in him somehow. The drug store just doesn't have enough business to keep her on. The owner of the store's husband made a drunken pass at Becky at Christmas and she wonders if this is the real reason she was let go. The University of Bow River thanks her for her interest in the program but regrets to inform her. Ian always sleeps curled away from her. They are familiar with the heat of each other's bodies. Familiar. Night after night. "But then they die anyway." With all the stories you've buried. With the eulogies and euphemisms your existence provides. Goddamn you, Ian.

FACULTY OF ARTS
DEPARTMENT OF HISTORY

Leaf Houri
403-581-3213
lhouri@ubowriver.ca

Dear Rebecca Burgess,

Your application for admission to the doctoral program in History and its supporting credentials have been carefully reviewed by the Admissions Committee. We regret to inform you that we are unable to offer you admission at this time.

We thank you for your interest in studying History at the University of Bow River, and wish you success in your future academic endeavours.

[signature]

Dr. Leaf Houri,
Graduate Chair, Department of History,
University of Bow River

IAN

She has rules for every clock. The clock in the bedroom is set 20 minutes early so she doesn't wake up late. Late for what? The clock on the stove is an hour behind because I can't figure out how to adjust for daylight savings. Or the other one, the opposite of daylight savings, whatever that one is called. Her watch and her phone have rules. The clock in the TV room is set to Ontario time and stands next to the phone so she knows what time it is "back home" for when she calls her mother. Which she never does. I have to do math to tell time. Add an hour. Subtract two hours. After two watchbands broke catching on stretchers I figured out that I can't really wear a watch, so I rely on the rules of the clocks. When the TV room clock tells me that I'm nearly two hours late for work I head in.

Jarrington's Family Funeral Parlour hired me as a transfer agent and trainee funeral director five years ago as I was finishing my Funeral Service Direction degree at Mount Royal College (they've since become Mount Royal University and the alumni association seem kind of bitchy about that fact). Corporate funeral homes are steadily eating up more and more of the market, but the family-owned and family-operated funeral home is still common. It's very difficult to get ahead in the Death Industry if your last name isn't printed on the door. Five years later and I'm still technically a trainee. Jarrington's son, who is so stupid Jarrington is afraid to retire despite being about a thousand years old, is now running the "front of house" operations. That's how this business works. Whatever. I'm doing "back of house" work today—that is, the stuff the public and the customers don't ever see. The preparation rooms, the embalming, the cremation retorts. When I'm in the parlour and not in the van I'm generally stuck in the back of house, which really means the basement. Away from the sunlight and the recently bereaved in the showrooms. This suits me. Jarrington and his son can push the caskets, never called coffins, and the receptacles. It is okay to say urn when they are ready to buy, people are okay with the idea of *owning* an urn, but otherwise we try to call it a receptacle as some people aren't okay with the idea of their dad actually *being* in an urn. You wouldn't think there would be enough business to support all the funeral homes here in the west, but death, as Jarrington likes to joke (only in the basement, never in the earshot of bereaved) is a growth industry. The population is getting older, he says. He doesn't cite his sources. No one questions him. He's pretty old. I don't mind the basement. We can listen to music and Vince is usually working. I like Vince, he is a nerd. It's always nerds who work the basements. I've transferred to a few different homes in neighbouring towns (ones that don't have vans available or are understaffed call Jarrington—he gets a commission farming me to them), and it's always nerds who work their basements, too. D&D and X-Men comics and Trekkers—not Trekkies, Vince snapped at me once. If you've got no social skills then work with the dead. It seems kind of on the nose and I said that to Vince once and he said fuck off. But it works the way it works, so fine. Work with the dead. Hide from the light like trolls. It means no one bothers me most of the day and I can listen to Vince's CDs all day. Seems fine. Vince likes indie rock and mostly I can stand it so we get along. He invited me to play Dungeons and Dragons with his group once but I died the first night and Vince never mentioned them playing again, so I guess I didn't go over well with the nerd group. I just couldn't take it that seriously. The lives they'd made up for themselves. Who cares? One guy who was an elf or something insisted that we refer to him by his character's name, which was like ten syllables long. A minotaur gored me and Vince's friend wouldn't heal me until I asked "in character" for a healing spell. I didn't. He let me die. Vince is okay, though. He likes his escapism but he doesn't take it so seriously that I have to deal with it. We can be in the here and now. Mostly we just talk about music or sports or, rarely, women. Mostly we just grunt agreements and work quietly. Every once in a while we get a beer together. Usually just one. I feel guilty if I don't go home to Becky right away and Vince has a standing *World of Warcraft* group that he doesn't like to keep waiting.

"Hi, Ian. What's good?"

Hey Vince.

"Swinger in the prep room. You wanna start the prep? Lig is still on it."

Fuck. Yeah okay.

When a suicide is brought in the government coroner has to examine it before we can prep the body. When it's a hanging, the transfer agents or the cops or whoever collects the body is required to leave the ligature around the neck until the coroner examines it. That means the rope or the bed sheets or the sturdy old-fashioned orange extension cord is still on the body when we start work. Once when I was gurneying a transfer past the parents, the cord slipped out from under the sheet. Swinging. And the father groaned deep in his chest with a noise that I still remember and sometimes think I hear. I avoided eye contact. I got the transfer in the van. I don't like the ligature jobs.

If Vince wants me to prep a suicide, that means the coroner has already been in and signed off. I enter the prep room, breathe in the chemical tang of the room. The putrification of death has no chance in a funeral home. The things we use to create the illusion of life are much more powerful. We preserve the body in a moment that never happened. When I'm done the family will say, "he looks so peaceful." "It's like he's sleeping." They will peek at the shirt collar, looking for bruising on the neck. Signs of death on a body that will look healthier than any of those gathered to see him. They will not see any damage.

His organs will have been removed from his body. So peaceful. Jarrington is expensive and we do good work. The teenager-cum-suicide-cum-transfer-cum-remains doesn't look all that much at peace, just at this particular moment. I have work to do. I will erase the damage. I will rouge the cheeks. I will even do his hair if Vince is working on something else. He's better at the style stuff than I am, I'll admit it. But first I will cut the rope off the transfer's neck. First I will drain the fluids from his body and replace them with preservatives. Or I will start, anyway. Vince is the prep guy and I'm only a trainee. They let me do some of it for my training (or because Vince is lazy) but mostly I only assist. I'm qualified for prep work but Vince isn't going anywhere. The best I can hope for is that business stays good and when Jarrington finally retires his son needs me full time to help out. I'd take over most of the funeral direction and he'd run the business end. And probably run it into the ground without his old man to help. This is best-case scenario for me. But it's something. For now, though, the limbo of being an eternal trainee is comfortable enough. I make a little bit of money and I have a ton of experience now if opportunity ever presents itself. I could be making more money. Becky really needs to find a job.

This kid hung himself with his belt. The ligature here is a teenager's studded belt. I hope whatever fastens those studs to the belt doesn't stick out on the inside of the belt and pock up the neck. I'll have enough goddamn work there.

The vast majority of the remains that come to us through the coroner have had a glossectomy performed on them. This is the removal of the tongue and usually the glands, esophagus, parts or all of the soft tissues in the mouth and throat. I honestly don't know why. Vince said these tissues are easy to test for poison but this kid wasn't poisoned. It doesn't seem to matter what they died of, the coroner almost always takes the tongue. When I first learned all of this I thought about making a "dead men tell no tales" joke but I didn't know Vince that well. Didn't want to come off as a ghoul. Now I know it probably was the right call not to make the joke. There's no dead body joke you can make to someone in a funeral parlour that they haven't heard a thousand times. Everyone thinks they're the first to come up with a corpse fucker joke. It's the instinct to talk, again. To make a joke out of something that isn't funny. But it's the wrong impulse. The words don't fit the situation. Words aren't enough so just don't. What's the point in talking about it?

The stripped and sheet-covered body on the table was probably about 16. I glance at and then remove the hospital toe-tag. 15. Found last night. I note his tiny blue penis because even after five years I still always look. Once the preservative fluids are in him it will swell considerably. More considerably than you would expect. There is no joke you can make about this I haven't heard.

They didn't call a transfer; paramedics brought this one to the hospital although obviously the kid was DOA. Rigour already setting in when they hooked him down, I'd guess from the look of the neck. Officially pronounced dead in the hospital. That might help the parents. They can think their son died in a hospital. Not in the bedroom next to theirs. His music still playing when they found him. Friends still texting him after his body has gone stiff. I'll get an abdominal cavity aspiration started for Vince. I'm essentially going to put a big steel spike through the kid's chest and vacuum his guts out, really. The euphemism is lovely, though. Aspiration.

I'm glad I didn't get the call in for this one. Once they're a naked body on the table in here they don't bother me much but I have to admit, the young ones get in my head when I'm there for the transfer. I hate going into a room and seeing a girl's stuffed animals as I unpack the bag and set up the gurney. The father crying but not sure if he's supposed to offer to help. Half the time they hold the door for us. What do you do? You don't tell the grieving father that you've got it. You don't tell him anything. Avoid eyes. Avoid words. He holds it open and you grunt "thanks, buddy" like he's some guy who reminds you your gas tank cover is open after you fill up. Words are not helpful. My first transfer wasn't a kid, but a kid was there. She watched me wheel her mother out. The cops were asking her some questions and she shouldn't have been there when we brought the transfer out. But she was. And I looked her in the eyes when I—

But I'm not dealing with that now. This kid on the table stripped and removed from his life. Its life. This I can deal with. This is a job and meat. Two violent deaths in two days are not common in Coaldale. Jarrington draws some business from Lethbridge and outskirts and most of the towns and farmsteads east, but still. Small population of people and most of them try hard not to die and end up here. It's rare to do more than two funerals in a week. The old and shrivelled, the wasted or the bloated trickle in. They ride to Vince's prep room in the back of my van. The next of kin, shattered but stoic, in the showrooms upstairs. They were expecting this. At least on some level.

With young people, though, it's much worse. The shock and the anger. The sadness of the deaths has a viciousness attached to the sadness. Even Jarrington's idiot son doesn't try to upsell these families. Well. Not much. When the despair and the rage blast themselves out and defeat sets in, Jarrington and son will still probably recommend something from the Monarch line. They have bills to pay, too. Vince and I are cheap, but we're not free.

Suddenly I realize that this kid didn't walk into our prep room and lie down himself. I didn't transfer the body from the hospital to our basement. Who did?

Vince, who did the removal on the swinger from the hospital?

"Huh? Oh. Jarrington did it himself. He and the Coroner brought him in early. Then they went to breakfast."

Son of a bitch. I could have used the hours.

"Tell me about it."

Old Jarrington is a big man, bigger before age began to wither him. And he's not afraid to get his hands dirty, especially if it will save him a few bucks. I realize I didn't see the other black van when I pulled in this morning. I had no reason to notice.

Did they take the fucking van out to eat?

"Yeah I think so."

Jesus.

Most people won't know what the van is if they don't look at it too closely; it simply looks like a black van with tinted back windows and the Jarrington Family Funeral Home logo on the side. But for some reason taking a corpse wagon to breakfast seems weird. Jarrington and the county coroner are both older than stone and twice as tough, though. Between the two of them, there is not a single, solitary fuck given. Not a one to be had. I half suspect "breakfast" is gin on Jarrington's porch. It's a warm morning.

Gloves on. Scissors. Ligature removed as cleanly as possible. Really don't want to damage it; occasionally the police demand certain things taken with the transfers as evidence. Into a baggie and sealed. Labelled. If they aren't asked for, they sit in baggies in prep room storage for a year and get thrown out in spring cleaning. We could burn them in the retort, I suppose, but that somehow seems unholy. That's where people burn. Also, I guess that's not very ecological. Jarrington is always getting pissy phone calls about the pollution cremation causes.

We respect your opinion and share your concerns. However the industry is what it is and Jarrington's provides a service that our customers desire for their loved ones. When a better, greener solution is embraced by our customers, Jarrington Family Funeral Planning will be eager to adapt to suit the needs of our community.

Old Jarrington has this printed out next to the phone in his office in case anyone else has to take a call while he's out. It's in the same pile as the catalogue for the Monarch products and our service price guide.

Vince sticks his head in.

"Hey did you start the— " The steel spike penetrates and answers with a wet familiar sound just as he speaks. "Okay, great. I'll take over there. You wanna get the trays lined up?"

Sure.

I begin assembling the trays of tools and preservatives for Vince like a nurse laying out a surgeon's instruments. Well, not exactly like. Our patients never pull through. But they do leave looking better than they came in. This is better than doing paperwork upstairs or taking phone calls from environmentalists and bereaved. Making arrangements. Being micromanaged by Young Jarrington (twenty years older than me, bald, fat, stupid, and big but not as big as Old Jarrington). Showing numb people the gold trim and cushioned interior of the Eternité range of caskets.

"Hey, did the new guy really quit in the middle of a field yesterday?" Vince asks, surprising me out of my thoughts. He's bent over the kid on the table and I move the trays to where he can reach them without really looking.

Nate. Yeah. He did.

"His name was Nate? I thought it was something with a G."

I shrug. A few minutes without speaking. Vince's tools against flesh and the suction of the aspiration. I punch a gloved finger at the shitty CD player sitting on a low stainless steel table amidst drop sheets and packages of cosmetics. *Drive my car into the ocean.*

"Right on," says Vince, absently. "I was looking for that CD. Like last week."

I had it in the van. Sorry.

"I'm so in love with Kim Deal."

It is difficult not to be in love with Kim Deal.

We can talk like this because Kim Deal is not a real person. She is not in front of us on a table. She has existed in this song the same way for a long time. I collect the instruments as Vince finishes with them. Dispose of the ones that are single use and put the others back on the tray. I will wash them later. We go through quite a lot of bleach.

"Shit. If the new guy is gone I guess I'm riding shotgun if we get a call."

This used to be Young Jarrington's backup responsibility when we didn't have a second transfer agent. Turnover or budget—we often don't. But Young Jarrington has moved up in the world. Not enough that Old Jarrington actually trusts him, but enough so that it won't do to have him seen handling the transfers. Makes a bad impression for shaking hands and selling later.

Now he handles the money. The products. The bereaved. He won't be sent out to lift and Old Jarrington isn't allowed to send just one person. I'm sure he would if he could. He makes money on this place but there are a surprising number of funeral homes in the west. Lots of competition, he'll cut corners where he can. I'm glad the stricture is in place. Most people who die in the home do so in the bathroom. On the toilet or fallen over into the tub usually. It goes like this: giant man wakes up in the middle of the night and doesn't feel right. Pain in the chest and guts and uncomfortable. Sweating. Goes in to the bathroom to hide his suffering from his wife because if it's *not* a heart attack he'll be embarrassed if he wakes her up. Thinks a shit or a glass of water will help. Coronary on the toilet. Often when they finally realize how serious it is, they try to get up. Put a hand on the tub ledge for support and inevitably tumble half-in, half-out of the tub. 320 pound, 6 foot 4 inches of corn-fed farmer with rigour setting in so that you have to wrestle him in the crowded narrow space between tub and counter to try and get him out. I'm very glad Jarrington has to send someone else with me. But Vince hates transfers. Not because they disturb him emotionally like Nate; they just disturb his day. Like any nerd he wants to be left alone in his basement. He's not a Jarrington, and he's worked hard to run their back of house. To reach this present.

"I hope no one dies today," he says.

Me too.

"I'm way too busy."

Vince and I will finish the prep on this case and later today cremate the remains of the accident I transferred yesterday. Those remains are as prepared as possible given the circumstances. Those will not be displayed. Those are for the fire. Well, more fire. Stored in the sliding refrigerated trays against the east wall that rumbleslide out like deep filing cabinets. Vince is training me in embalming and cremation although I've been able to do both for years now. Like I said, positions are few and far between for non-family members who want to rise above the level of transfer agent or trainee. I assist Vince in his work. Kim Deal sings about mutilation. The workday passes.

At lunch I strip off my gloves and scrubs and walk outside. Stroll the few blocks to the sandwich shop on 16th street and take in the sun. Benny's Deli has a little patio outside the front door. Just a couple of cheap sets of aluminum patio furniture under some sun umbrellas. A young blonde girl looks up over bug-eye sunglasses at me. I had instinctively looked down her spaghetti-strapped tank top and quickly shift my eyes. Make for the door to Benny's.

"Hello," she says.

Hi.

"I know you, I think."

I stop and turn back to her. She looks about 20. Maybe. Pretty little oval face. Or mostly pretty. There's something about her that is just slightly off. A slight asymmetry maybe. I can't tell, I just see it. Heart shaped lips stained red. Eyes hazel as she pulls down the glasses to study my face. Too young to be someone I know. I recognize middle-aged people a lot when I'm out. People who have had to bury their parents. But rarely young people.

No, I don't think so.

"Yes, I do."

A pause, a moment while she thinks. I smile and try to think of an exit strategy. Really I just want to get a sandwich and sit by myself for a while.

"You took my mother."

Excuse me.

"When my father killed her. You came for the body. You looked at me as you wheeled her out. I remember you."

Oh.

Shit.

Thinking back takes me out of my comfort zone, the plodding but certain day-to-day, but my first transfer went like this. It was about five years ago. The girl must have been about 9 or 10. So not 20. 16 or 17. The bug-eyes make her look older. Or that's my excuse for looking down her top. Maybe I'm just a dirty old bastard. Anyway. A call came in from the police that there was a body to be extracted from a crime scene. Young Jarrington (fat and bald even five years ago) was training me and swore after he hung up the phone. Active investigation crime scenes, he said, are a pain in the ass. You have to sign in and out. You have to tiptoe around the damn place and deal with testosterone-machine cops barking at you. It's their show and they know it. I wasn't really nervous. Curious more than anything. I'd only seen the bodies used at the school. This was real, though. I was going to remove one from a crime scene. I wondered if it would be warm at all to the touch. How long ago had it—

I asked questions in the van.

Is it a murder?

"Probably. Cop sounded super pissed. Usually murders piss them off because they have to do a ton of work."

What?

"Some crimes they don't really have to do much. You get robbed they take some notes and say they'll keep a look out for patterns of similar robberies. If the stolen stuff turns up in a pawn shop or something maybe they investigate but really what are they gonna do? Go into random houses and see if your shit is in there? Naw. They just write some stuff down and go eat. But a murder? They can't get away with doing nothing for that. People get upset about murder."

Well. Yeah. I mean. It's murder. It's a person.

"It was. That reminds me. Don't refer to the deceased at the scene. Call it a transfer if you have to say anything. Try not to talk, especially to the cops. They'll be pissy. Just let me handle it. If it's a crime scene we probably won't have to worry about the family so I can tell you that stuff later."

Okay.

"You scared?"

Of what?

"Good answer."

The crime scene was a house. Just a house. A little brick two story just outside town. There was a garden and the lawn was mowed. It was all so normal except for the police cruisers with their cherries lit and wheeling in the driveway.

"Shit I know the guy who lives here," said Young Jarrington. "He works at the butcher shop."

A glowering cop standing at the front door came up to us as we unloaded the gurney from the back of the van. He stabbed a finger at the spot I was to sign. Talked to Young Jarrington briefly. Jarrington signed in three or four places. A copy for the funeral home was ripped from the clipboard. Young Jarrington tucked it in his breast pocket and turned to me.

"Transfer's in the kitchen."

We lifted the gurney up the front porch and entered the house. Two cops were talking gently to a young girl. Gangly tomboy with scraped knees poking out of her shorts. Dirty blonde hair in a lazy ponytail. She had grubby hands from playing outside and was clutching a Wonder Woman comic book while she tried to understand what the police kneeling in front of her were asking. She looked over the nearest cop's shoulder and met my eyes. When I stopped, the gurney rolled over my toe.

"That'll teach you. Keep it moving, kid." I pulled my eyes away from her hazel pierce. An unloaded gurney wasn't heavy, my toe was fine. But I felt her watch me. Back through the hallway. Into the kitchen.

The woman. The transfer was lying on the floor. Nothing was disturbed in the kitchen. There must not have been much struggle. She almost looked like she had slipped and fallen. Or died calmly, simply collapsing in her neat kitchen. Except that her throat was purple and crushed. Her blonde hair fell in thin wisps around the damage of her neck. A gob of blood thick around her mouth. Stray hairs tucked in the corner of her mouth and matting in the blood. Her eyes closed and restful but her face awful. No one dies beautifully, but I was not appalled. I thought of her daughter's eyes. Wondered if behind the lids this woman— If this transfer's eyes were hazel. Wanted to know what the body felt like. If she was warm.

"Whoa. Gloves! Always gloves, kid."

Right. Sorry.

I fished them from my back pocket. Remembered not to snap them when I pulled them up onto my forearm. The woman was light and we hefted her easily onto the stretcher. Hands under armpits. Head lolling back against my crotch briefly before we positioned her.

"Good," Young Jarrington whispered now, not wanting the cops or girl to hear us. "Good with the head. Always keep the head up. You can let an arm or a leg hit the ground if you slip but you gotta support the head. A head knocking against the ground sounds exactly like you think it will. And everyone in the house knows what you've done if you let that hit."

Young Jarrington drew a sheet up over what used to be a woman. Loosely tucked the sheet in. Don't want it to fall off but also don't really want to outline the shape underneath too clearly, either. Euphemism.

"That kid shouldn't be here. They should have taken her somewhere. How the fuck are we supposed to work with her sitting there?"

He was worried about us working.

They must be waiting for family. Someone to take her.

"Yeah, maybe. Shit, I hope it wasn't the husband. He's not a bad guy. It's always the husband, though."

Really?

"Yeah. Women get killed in their own homes it's always the man. If there's a man. Boyfriend or husband or whatever."

We uh. We can't just wait in here until they go, can we?

"No. They'll want us to sign back out. I hate wheeling this out there with her there. Well. But we better go. If they are waiting on more family it'll be even worse if we stall. It'll be awkward as hell, plus I hate to be callous or whatever, but we won't sell them anything if they see the body before the service. They'll want it cremated just to get rid of the memory."

And so we wheeled the old gurney back through the front room. Now laden, one wheel squeaked against the hardwood. Squawking like a nightmare. We've replaced that gurney since. The police stopped talking but didn't look back. Shoulders hunched up towards ears. The girl looked. Her hazel eyes taking in Young Jarrington, me, the sheeted gurney wheeling the body of her—

The transfer. This time I looked away.

I call home and tell Becky I'll be late coming home from work. When she asks why I tell her that I'm going to hang out with Vince for a little while. She seems annoyed, but she buys it. I don't know why I lie. I just can't find words to tell her the truth without it sounding like I am doing something wrong. Something very strange. I'm suddenly guilty. As if the girl and I share something. At the sandwich shop the girl had said:

"When my father killed her. You came for the body. You looked at me as you wheeled her out. I remember you."

Oh shit.

Oh shit. I uh. Just um.

I sputtered. What should I have said here? I looked helplessly around me. Looked into the sandwich shop. At people eating their lunches and not having horrifying conversations. The guy behind the counter in the sandwich shop's mother died last winter. Jarrington had let me handle some of the funeral arrangements. I sometimes wonder if getting my lunches here is a painful reminder for him but he never seems to recognize me. Also in all the handshaking when I'd served him he'd given me about twenty business cards and coupons. The girl speaks and brings me back.

"Oh I'm sorry. Are you on your lunch break?"

Yeah. Uh yes.

"Full morning of collecting the dead?"

Look. I—

I wanted to apologize to her. I don't know why. Is that what you do? This I was not trained for. I know the patter and euphemism for the recently bereaved. But this?

"No, that wasn't nice of me. When do you get off work?"

Oh. Uh. Five or six-ish. Depending.

"Depending on what?"

On how fast the remains…uh.

"How fast the remains what? Burn?"

Well. Yeah.

Stupid. I swallowed but didn't look away from her this time. I'd been panicked into the truth. Euphemism and the service of keeping the public from knowing what they don't need to know failed me. She seemed unphased.

"Alright. Well come back here when you're done. I'll come back and wait for you."

Okay.

Something about the way she said it left no room for argument. Of course I would come back and talk to this woman… girl whose mother's remains I had transferred five years ago. After her father strangled the woman to death in their kitchen. Of course. This is absolutely what I would do.

I backed into the sandwich shop. Stood in line and tried not to look for her out of the corner of my eye. Somehow bought a sandwich I don't remember ordering and left. She watched me the whole time. Hazel above the rim of those big glasses. Her face a half-smirk or sneer, I couldn't tell which. I retreated down the street with my sandwich and felt her eyes.

"My name is Athene," she had called after me. I flinched as if she had struck me between the shoulder blades and kept walking.

I won't go. It's stupid to go. Probably unprofessional. Definitely super weird. But now as I mop the prep room and watch Vince double check the seal of the cremation retort, I find myself thinking about what to say when I call home. What lie to tell Becky. Why lie? Because how do I expla—

"Yo. Wake up."

What? Sorry Vince.

"Do you?"

Do I what? I'm sorry. I really spaced out.

Her name is Athene. Vince laughs at me.

"Do you have the clear from Jarrington?"

Oh. Oh the forms. Yeah hold on. Here.

"He signed it but there isn't anything here about next of kin."

No. But if it's signed we go ahead, right?

"Well, yeah, but if there are family who want to view the…"

I don't think anyone is going to want to see. That.

We both look at the retort. Stainless steel and heavy

handles. Seals and gauges. Family who insist on viewing the cremation are always surprised there isn't a window. Windowed retorts are rare these days and they fire at a much lower temperature. They take forever. We fire around 1900 Fahrenheit. Ash and bits of bone fragment in only a couple of hours. They see their loved one go in but they don't stay in the back of house while they burn. Jarrington leads them to the parlour. Expertly steers them towards their waiting party. Offers drinks. Nods understandingly. Presses hands. He is everyone's grandfather as their loved one becomes our transfer. Becomes ash and melted fat. Muscles and skin curl in the heat; the corpse will sometimes try to sit up from the contraction. At the same time Jarrington tactfully finalizes plans. Are they still happy with the music selected to play as the rest of the mourners file in? Frank Sinatra's "My Way" is nearly a given when the deceased is a male of a certain fiscal bracket. Children most often get lullabies. Women are harder to predict. Are they happy with the imperial purple-trimmed black drape over the table the receptacle will adorn? There is also this gold with black. Here is a tasteful walnut. Most cremations are handled before the service, preferably the day before like this one. But when they want to view sometimes they make us cram everything into one day. I don't envy Jarrington his babysitting of the bereaved while we burn their departed down and sweep them into a container. I call home. Lying to Becky about where I'll be. I remember the purple of Athene's mother's neck. The blooded pout of lips and hair. I don't wear a watch and my phone is next to the computer in the other room so I ask Vince for the time. We should be done a little after five as long as the transfer burns quickly.

Her name is Athene. Vince fires the retort.

BECKY

Annoyed she stabs the phone back onto the cradle charger. Of course. Go out for beers with Vince. She resents more that she feels she has to structure her day around his comings and goings than she does the actual fact that he will be home late. Becky is hungry. No point in waiting for him to get home to eat, then. Make something? No. She hates cooking. She hates cooking for him but she's home and he's at work. She often feels she should. And hates the obligation and the guilt. It's nothing he's said. But he expects it. Or she expects that he expects it. Chases this around her mind and gets more angry. Also more hungry. Pizza? She doesn't know what she wants. Thai or Indian maybe but the options in this town are pretty limited. Fuck it.

    Becky retrieves her cell phone. Why do they even *have* a landline? But she can't tell Ian to get rid of it. Can't tell him what to do with *his* money. She texts some friends to see what they are doing for dinner. She has barely talked to them lately, but she will go out, too. She wonders where Ian and Vince are going. The sports bar near the funeral home, probably. She suddenly wants very much to avoid seeing him when she's out. She finds this perverse. Viv texts back that she's not free. No answer from Jenn. Becky feels fussy and restless. Leans against the kitchen counter and stares at nothing. Her phone rings but it is Ian's mother. She lets it go to voicemail. Let the horrid old spider leave a message. She waits a few minutes to hear from Jenn but still nothing. Five more minutes. Fuck it, she thinks again. I don't have to go out with someone. I can just go. Strange how much of a hermit she has become. Not working has dominated her life. This house has become a boundary. She only goes out to resupply it. To serve the house. She picks her car keys from the bowl by the front door. She leaves her phone in the bowl.

Becky backs the car out of the gravel drive in front of the squat brown two-bedroom she and Ian rent in west Coaldale. Well, Ian rents, she thinks bitterly. Her name on the lease too, but her dwindling money no longer contributing. She will need to find something soon. She waits while the early commuters pull past her on their way home from work and swings backwards into the street. Waves to a neighbour. About the only perk of Ian's working for a funeral home is that Jarrington has a small fleet of black sedans in addition to the vans and the monstrous hearse. Old Jarrington doesn't mind the staff driving the cars as long as they keep the tank filled, and so usually Ian is able to leave his car at home in case Becky wants it. His car. She feels the hydraulic squeeze of brakes and knows it is his.

She never needed a car living in the city. Had not bothered getting her driver's license until they moved west—an ordeal; she failed the driving test twice—and she found little pleasure in driving. Maybe if the car was *hers*. But very little is hers anymore. Her life has shaped itself around him. Even now, these words, these thoughts she angrily stirs and turns over define her against him. She exists in this place because of him. It is not his fault, exactly, but sometimes she hates him for it. For his hunger and his smell on clothing in the hamper. The flecks of his beard in the sink. The fact that none of it is malicious or purposeful from him makes it worse, somehow. He isn't aware of anything in her life. When he comes home he seems surprised if she has moved positions from when he left. He asks "What did you do today?" in a tone that implies he might believe she simply pops out of existence when he closes the door. You did nothing today, he accuses. Or he doesn't. Putting malice into their conversations has become something of a hobby for both of them.

Things were supposed to have gone differently. Like everyone else, she realises, but does not care. It is hard for her to accept the life she lives because it seems so temporary. Stopgap and therefore unreal. She cannot resolve herself to it. This was not the plan. She expected and still expects happily ever after.

She's not sure what this stopping-off point is. How many people, she wonders, die waiting for their real life to begin? Then she chides herself for allowing herself this kind of mawkish idiocy. She would mock Ian viciously for anything similar. But still. Was the future a happily ever after or is it like *The Jetsons*—everyone still bored, still wanting something more, just with better cars and bitchy robot maids. Ian's 2005 Corolla churning dust on the county road beneath her does not feel particularly utopian. Weren't we supposed to have flying cars by now? With a purring space-aged putter and clean white rings emitted. Have solved hunger. Achieved world peace and clean energy. Or something. Well I guess we fucked that one up, she thinks. Alberta and driving when she didn't really need to go out. Oil crisis be damned. Okay, she thinks, this is also on me. She merges onto the highway.

Suddenly Becky realizes she has begun leaving the limits of Coaldale. She had meant to cruise downtown (the Toronto girl still within her winces at calling the tiny strip of pubs and shops on Main Street/20th Ave "downtown") and look for a place to eat, but now she is heading west on Crowsnest Hwy.

CALGARY—220 KM

Alright, she thinks. This is on me, too.

IAN

Walking, I turn the corner where Benny's Sandwiches is and maybe she won't be there. Why would she be there? Kid like that. Better things to do than talk to the man who took her mother. Man in his 30s.

She's alarming. Waifish or impish or something-ish. Shorter than Becky but thinner. Angles more than curves but pretty. She will look like her mother. Her dead mother. Jesus Christ what is wrong with me.

Should be out with boys. At the mall with friends. Something. She remembered my face. Why would she come? Why am I going? She won't be there. But I know that she will be. And as I approach Benny's patio I see that she is. She's reading a book, looks up over it as she notices me approaching but goes back to reading. I walk up, stand nervously for a moment. Touch the back of the seat across from her but don't pull it out. She glances up and smiles at me.

"Half a minute," she says. Goes back to reading.

I pull the chair out and it scrapes horrible, metal runners rake the patio like Titanic on iceberg. I grimace and sink into the chair. The traffic on the street seems to have quieted simply to make my every move louder. I shift in the chair and it squeaks. She keeps reading.

She's reading *Lolita*. Jesus. Come on. I mean, I've never

actually read it but I understand what it means. And just. Really? This feels contrived but I watch her lips as she reads. I do. She reaches the end of a section and dog-ears a page. Closes the book.

"Hello."

Hi.

"I'm surprised you came."

Oh. Uh. Yeah. I did. Or I mean. Me too.

Blather like an idiot. What to say here? I felt I should? I somehow owe it to her? I have a really strange and vague guilt that she has somehow tapped into? No I don't want to say that. Obvious as her book. If I had realized she really didn't expect me to show I might have taken the out and not come.

"Well," she says, "should we go have a drink?"

Are you old enough to? Can you drink?

She laughs at me. Okay. Fine.

Okay. Fine. Let's get a drink.

She hooks a messenger bag off the back of her chair and puts her book inside. Stands and settles the strap of the bag between her breasts. I don't think she notices me notice.

"You didn't tell me your name."

Oh. Right.

"So. What is your name?"

Oh Jesus. Yeah, sorry. It's Ian. I'm Ian.

"Do I make you nervous, Ian."

Kind of. No. No, not really. Laugh it off. Haha. Oh I'm just a bit out of it. Had a long day. Coming down with something. Any number of answers. Does she make me nervous.

You horrify me.

We settle into a booth at Jack's pub and the waitress doesn't blink as Athene orders a glass of red wine. Or I guess the server. I don't think you're supposed to say waitress anymore although waiting sounds preferable to serving to me. In any case Athene goes unchallenged as she orders the house red. When I was underage I snuck into a bar exactly once. I was terrified the whole time that a bouncer would lay a meaty hand on my shoulder at any moment. I drank half a beer and told my friends I had to bail. Sudden migraine.

The server waits patiently for me now and I order a Stella.

"Sorry, we don't have Stella."

Fuck that's right. Pat's has Stella. I don't go out a lot and when I do it's always the same two places. Not that there are a ton of choices in Coaldale worth going to. I think Jack's has Wild Rose beers.

Um. Do you have Velvet Fog?

"Yup, sure do. You want a bottle or a pint?"

A pint, please.

Maybe I should have ordered a bottle. Maybe I shouldn't drink as much as a pint. The server smiles and retreats. Athene leans over the table at me. Dark in here and her huge eyes eerie as they move from shadow.

"I pictured you as more of a whiskey man."

I have a rye and Coke now and then.

"Scotch. Neat."

Straight booze makes me kind of sick.

"A long day among the dead and scotch to steel your nerves. A real western feel to you."

Um. Not so much.

"Beer is okay. That's still fairly manly. But Stella? What are you, a French painter? A redneck who *wants* to be a French painter?"

I think it's Belgian. I'm supposed to be manly?

"I'm not sure. Just the image I've created of you."

She has created an image. Of me. Uh.

Uh.

"I was twelve the last time I saw you. You looked manly to a twelve-year-old."

I force a laugh. Is this right? I can't navigate this.

Oh. Well I'm sorry to disappoint you.

"I didn't say I was disappointed." She basically purrs this at me. Oh come on. I almost feel bad for her. This show she's putting on. She's trying too hard, except for the fact that it's working on me. I'm here. She sinks back from the table and out of the light as our drinks arrive. I thank the server.

"You're welcome," she says. "Did you guys want to start a tab, or…"

Oh. Uh no, I'll just settle—

"Yes," Athene interrupts sweetly. "Let's just start a tab, honey, we're celebrating." I blink and stare dumbly. The server smiles in a way that makes me hate every tooth in her head.

"Oh, what are you two celebrating?"

"We've been apart for a long time," Athene says, looking at me. Smiles too, but smaller. Sharper. "We're finally catching up."

"I'll just start that tab, then," the server says and levels an exaggerated wink at me. "You two be good over here in the dark…" and she disappears back towards the bar. This time Athene doesn't lean forward. Small pale hand disembodied appears beneath the hanging light and slowly takes up the glass of wine. Grasps the bowl with delicate fingers. Her fingernails a chipped 17-year-old's purple. Is holding the glass by the bowl right for red wine? The stem for white? It has something to do with body heat. Or tannins. Or. Wait, what are tannins again? I can never remember. I don't drink wine often. Christmas parties at the funeral home when everyone is drinking wine I'll have a glass. But half the time we're drinking out of Styrofoam cups Young Jarrington pulled out of a supply closet, so the stem/bowl thing is generally not an issue. Wine gives me a headache, anyway. Her hand moves the glass towards her lips in the semi-darkness. Lips part. I more imagine than see. I realize I'm watching her move and that we've gone quiet. In the dim booth it's hard to tell if she's staring back at me. It makes me uneasy not to know where she is looking. Flustered I stammer the first thing that comes to mind.

Do you uh. Do you usually not get ID'd when you go to bars? Or uh do you go a lot. Or. You know. Some.

Stupid. God I sound stupid. She's 14 years younger than I am. I did the math while I swept the basement at Jarrington's.

"Sometimes," she shrugs. "I have a good fake if so. I drink with older men and I don't order girly drinks. So that helps."

Older men. She drinks with men.

Right. Well I guess there's something to that.

We go quiet again. The shitty speakers behind the bar across the room feebly attempt to fill the air with decades-old rock.

So.

I have nothing to follow it with. She grins like predation. Her bright teeth dimmed beyond the lamp. Redness of the wine darkened as it rises to her lips. Finally, she leans forward again into the light. Cleavage across the table and I try not to glance. I glance. Disappointed in myself for a small, slow moment as eyes flick back. Again.

"Let's talk about my family, Ian."

I don't know your family.

I say it quickly. Too quickly and something like rage crosses her face for an instant and is gone. Shark smile returns. I'm not sure I didn't imagine the spasm of anger. A monstrous beauty.

"That's true in a way. Although you did give my mother a ride once. That was kind of you."

I just. It's a transfer. It's a job.

"Is that all it is?"

Well, or I mean. It's a career, right? Or it's something that I can make a career. It's a stepping stone. It's better than slinging hamburgers.

"Slinging corpses is better."

Okay, look.

"No, I'm sorry. I just don't understand, I think. And I mean, I've had a while to think about it, right? About you. What you did that day. And I know that was just a pick-up or whatever to you, just a job, but—"

We call it a transfer. We. We have a lot of names for things. Euphemisms.

"Transfer. Transference. Interesting. Okay. Okay, well I get that. I get that it was just another day at the office to you, but—"

Well actually it—

And I stop. Stupid. Don't. Don't get into this, don't establish some kind of connection. You're drinking fast from nervousness. She's cute or maybe just different and you've had your little look. Make nice, comfort her like you do all the bereaved and go home to Becky.

"What, Ian?"

Her eyes drill hazel into me. Little flyaway frizzes of her hair escape her ponytail. Her lips wet in low light and her eyes not.

It, uh. It wasn't really just another transfer. I mean, maybe it was but I didn't know that.

"What does that mean?"

That was the first transfer I was on. That was my first day on the job.

"Really?"

Yeah. I actually remember it, too. Everything about it.

"But you didn't recognize me. I guess I've changed since then."

Your eyes, I did. I remembered those.

"Really?"

Stop. Stop now.

Well, yeah. They're a nice colour. I mean. Just, I noticed.

And she sits back and crosses her arms. Did I just scumbag on a girl based on a shared history of having taken her mother's body? I drain my beer. Start to shift. She leans forward and touches my hand. Two fingers and thumb lightly touch the ridge of my knuckles.

"Thank you for telling me that. I know you probably think that this is weird, or whatever, but this actually helps me."

Oh. Okay I just.

And I am king asshole. I hadn't really considered that what she wanted here was *help*. She's a kid and her mom was killed.

That makes sense. There is no part of that that does not make sense and I constructed this whole little scenario where it's about *me*. What the hell is wrong with me?

"I hadn't ever seen a dead body before that day."

You saw her?

"I—I found them. My father was sitting at the kitchen table with his back to, to what he had done. He asked me to call the police and then he never said anything else to me. I called and they came and you came."

I'm so sorry.

"So many people came. The police took him. Then sat me down. Asked me things. I didn't understand what was going on. Later they said I was hysterical but by the time you showed up I had gone into shock, I think. They talked and talked but I just sat there. The way he did. They brought me candy and comic books and they kept calling me 'sweetheart.'"

Jesus.

"'Try and remember now, sweetheart. Sweetheart, did your daddy ever— ' it just went on and on. And then you came."

I say nothing. She needs to work through this. Okay, I get that. I don't necessarily want to sit through her talking therapy, but I understand this, now. This need to talk. But I can let her do this. Just say nothing. Nod for her.

"And you took her."

Nothing.

"And I hated you for that."

She leans forward again. Those eyes but not wet still. Crushing.

"More than him. What he did. I hated you for taking her."

PART 2
THE HISTORY OF PARABOLAE

the texts of literature and those of history are equally fair game
—LINDA HUTCHEON

BECKY

The story went or maybe goes like this. Becky settles the car between white paint lines in a parking lot at the University of Bow River. The school she was not good enough to study at. She had come here to prep for her first application to the doctoral program in history when she and Ian had first moved to Alberta. But her application had been rushed. She could have put more time in, but with the move and the sudden beginning of a new life, the application was half-assed. She consoled herself with the time constraint being responsible for her failure until another year had gone by and another thin envelope with the University of Bow River logo—jumping deer and Latin—had arrived.

> *Dear Rebecca Burgess,*
>
> *Your application for admission to the doctoral program in History and its supporting credentials have been carefully reviewed by the Admissions Committee. We regret to inform you that we are unable to offer you admission at this time. We thank you for your interest in studying History at the University of Bow River, and regret*

And so on. Again. But the "at this time" had given her hope after the initial despair and black dungeon bender of binge drinking and insomnia. At this time. And so she would try again. Try harder. She would put together a completely new proposal. Examine a different era and do personal research. Something. Her grades were good. Well, her Master's grades were good. She'd drunk a lot and fucked around in undergrad. But she'd made it into the Master's program and there she had excelled. Perhaps the M.A. from the University of Windsor did not carry much weight in the rest of Canada. The school had a bad reputation; really the city had a bad reputation. Becky had loved it, though. It wasn't as big or exciting as Toronto but Detroit was right across the river and there was always something happening. She loved the old ivy-covered buildings of the university, the mansions along Riverside Drive built by bootleggers with dirty money. She loved early morning runs through the sculpture garden by the Ambassador Bridge. Detroit looming and yet gleaming across the water.

"Dear Becky," she breathes to herself as she picks her way between cars in the University of Bow River parking lot, "we regret to inform you that your proposal does not indicate that you are a dyke or a native and so the department doesn't think we can get scholarship money from the university for you." Becky immediately feels like a monster for thinking this way. She stops to tie her shoelace and angles herself towards the quad. She desperately wants something else to be responsible for her failure, though. A reason, any reason, other than she was simply not good enough. Smart enough. It is easier to blame bureaucracy, reverse discrimination, bias against the smaller schools she'd done her undergrad work at, department politics. Anything. Other than hope and failure in a repeating arc.

Becky had gotten a general sense of the campus' layout when she had visited for her last kick at the doctoral can. She is pretty sure she can find the library, even not having been here for a year. She could have checked her phone, but she left it behind. The fall chill gives her a slight shiver and she zips up her hoodie. Shivering in May. In Windsor, Becky realizes, her friends will be opening their pools soon.

As she walks she watches students moving lazily between buildings. Lounging on the grass or beneath trees despite the cool. Probably born and bred Albertans who don't feel the cold, she thinks. Becky passes a group of boisterous young men in baseball caps and leather jackets. Each one tall and gorgeous. Trim and young. Becky momentarily gawks. She'd been seeing the same few people day after day in her housebound life in Coaldale. She had nearly forgotten the pleasures of campus life. None of the young men pay any attention to her. No heads turn as she passes. She is dressed for sitting around the house—baggy grey hoodie and dirty blue jeans. Hair in a loose mess on top of her head and beat up messenger bag instead of purse slung over her shoulder. She was not concerned a moment before. Suddenly she feels self-conscious. The idea of appearing attractive to men nearly ten years younger than she is becomes important to some reptile part of her brain. She recognizes this in herself and resents it, but allows her mind to continue. She looks back over her shoulder at the wall of retreating twenty-one-year-old asses. Athletic and poured into skinny jeans. When was the last time she'd been shamelessly hit on by a clerk? A bag boy or bank teller? Did the few male friends she had left occasionally fall asleep thinking about her? Their fists balled around—Maybe, she thinks. There was a time they would have. In Coaldale, at the pharmacy she had worked at, with Ian, with her small group of mostly thirty-something, mostly married and kid-having friends, her 29 years had felt young. Here she feels old. Not ancient, because that would be noteworthy. But old enough to go unnoticed. The middle stages of time. Not even middle-aged, with the weight that idea carries, just blank. No longer relevant, but not quite history. Not that dignified. Becky tugs on her topknot of hair and turns away from the young men. Fuck it. They look like a bunch of fucking date-rapist fratboy assholes anyway. She is again annoyed at herself for looking at herself through other people's eyes. *Quod influit per nos transierunt.*

Now, as she arrives at the building where she remembers assembling research materials last year, Becky is surprised to discover it is no longer a library. A new, digital library has been built. Most of the research materials she wants are available in the Crowchild Digital Library, she is told. On computer. As she crosses the modern walkway of glass and steel between the old library and the new, Becky hums softly to herself. Meet George Jetson. His boy, Elroy.

No, that can't be right. Is Elroy introduced second? He is. Jane is last. She takes George's wallet and future bubble scooters down to the astro shopping centre. The kitschy, schlocky sexism of the future. Progress. Becky has enough money for gas back to Coaldale. She will worry about everything else later. In the future.

She allows herself to be briefly amused by the irony of history only available digitally before becoming confused and intimidated by the Crowchild Library. The library of the future, a framed newspaper clipping on the wall says. Daughter Judy. Jane, his wife. Becky speaks to a librarian and learns that some books are available only to librarians. They are still being catalogued for the new library. Becky is told she can request anything, though, and the articles she wants can be scanned and sent to her student webmail. Does she have her student ID with her? No. She does not.

Becky does not know what articles to request. She had planned on browsing shelves. Seeing which books leapt out while she browsed the section. Becky's loose concept is to write about the Prohibition Era in Canada and the States. The smuggling across the Great Lakes. Many of the books relating to *that*, she is told, have yet to be processed. Becky finds the future difficult.

Eventually she manages to collect a small armful of books and journals peripherally related to her study. Some material on the smuggling between Montana and Alberta. Liquor trade with Natives. Articles railing against hundred-year-old laws that hamper movement across provincial borders for some reason. Some few things on the history she wants. Some look more promising than others, but she takes what she can get. The stacks in Windsor had been small, but they had felt like what Becky had thought stacks *should* feel like. Suitably dungeon-like, shabby, and private enough to feel like an escape into a world composed only of research. A romantic, if inconvenient, world of books and dust. Here the new bookshelves gleam with the sun pouring in through the glass. Beautiful undergraduates lounge everywhere in comfortable stuffed chairs with cups of gourmet coffee. She lugs the books and journals to a quiet corner of the third floor and sits with them. She watches the late Calgary sunset. Refraction. All this glass and gleaming steel is vaguely disconcerting to Becky. Her love of ivy and brick find no purchase on the newer, richer buildings of the Bow River campus. The glass and steel of *The Jetsons* was worthwhile, but here it just seems too real. But the sun across the quad, the shadows of trees and the dazzle of light through glass pleases her. She aches to be a part of this place. The life of the academy, the shape of a life she imagines, even a too-real academy she feels disconnected from in time and place. She had expected this for herself and she wants it now. She misses her massive lakes, marshlands, fruit belt. The Detroit River that smugglers drove shipments of whiskey across in cheap, disposable jalopies when the river froze. The booze worth more than the cars or the drivers so the crates were packed to float should the car break through the ice and be lost. The crates, at least, could be saved. Men with hats and guns. Women smuggling liquor in brassieres and garters. Essex County feeding Al Capone. Becky escapes Alberta.

IAN

A few beers in now. Had meant to stop at one but Athene orders us drinks anytime the server gets within earshot. Athene has become less scary, which helps. She leans forward constantly, asks me questions about myself. Flatters me. Her smile seems more like a smile as we talk and less like a shark's grin. She dribbles her wine slightly and licks her lips. Like *Lolita*, this is on the nose, but a few pints in I'm drawn to it. No angry texts from Becky yet and I haven't said anything to make me a scumbag. Well, more of a scumbag. I've been looking but barely. If talking helps this girl resolve some things, it's a good thing I think. I'm maybe letting myself off the hook here. Athene, now telling me about the University of Calgary. She's just finished high school and will be going to Calgary in September. Sociology. I think about Becky's failed attempts to get into Bow River but I don't mention Becky. Scumbag. Instead I slowly and methodically fold a napkin into an origami crane. I fuck these up about half the time and this one comes out looking slightly defective but serviceable. As far as paper birds go, it certainly is one.

"Cute."

Yeah. I have a real talent.

"I can't do anything like that."

It's not hard. I kind of fucked this one up.

Athene makes a gun out of her thumb and forefinger and shoots at my bird. Bang. I tip it over so it rests on one misfolded wing and its beak. That's okay. I hate birds.

"Can you make a hawk?"

I don't think so.

"An owl?"

I'm mostly limited to the crane. Or, uh. A little boat I guess.

Athene picks up the bird and considers it. I drink quietly and watch the bar slowly fill up. A few faces I recognize but don't really know. A middle-aged man nods at me solemnly as he passes towards the washroom. Olive green baseball cap shading a face I can't place. Judging by attitude and age I most likely transferred one of his parents. Athene absently frets at the paper crane. Slowly shreds it at the edges. The quiet hangs heavy and I still have half a beer left. I could drink up, settle and leave. Say it was nice meeting her. Or meeting her again. No maybe don't say that. I don't really want to pound half a pint though. And she looks up at me. Hazel pierce. I say something else instead.

So, uh. Why sociology?

"People fascinate me."

Oh yeah? That's cool. I'm not really a people person I don't think.

"Right business."

Ouch. But said without venom.

Well, yeah. If you like people, though, it's a good call. Sociology, I mean.

"I don't like people."

Excuse me?

"I don't want to study people because I *like* them."

Oh. For a job then I guess. It's a tough market.

"No. I want to know people so I can better consume them."

I spit my drink. I didn't think people actually did that. Like, you see it on TV but I've never actually spit a drink before. Spat a drink? I'm never sure. Drink comes out, in any case. Athene passes me the decimated crane and I mop up my mess with its frayed corpse.

Sorry.

Athene shrugs.

Consume them. Like. Okay yeah I don't know what—

"There are consumers and there are the consumed. People succeed in life by consuming others. Undermining them. Making them fail. Taking advantage of their weaknesses. It's like animals, right? I want to consume."

You don't really believe that.

"Of course I do. It's about as natural as anything else people can do."

That's awful. That's just. You're so young.

"Everyone is young until they're not. But the world runs on malice. And I want to learn how to make use of mine."

Okay.

"Okay."

I look at the clock over the bar. Jesus Christ.

"How's your drink?"

BECKY

In 1923 Roy A. Haynes, National Prohibition Director for the United States, came to Detroit. On seeing the Detroit River and Windsor across it, he said: "the Lord probably could have built a river better suited for rum-smuggling, but the Lord probably never did."

The difference between then and now is becoming less important. Less pronounced, perhaps, if not less important. It bleeds it bleeds it bleeds together. Here and there because there is the same as here except it's someplace else. Time is like that, maybe. Routine just in different clothes. It doesn't matter. The problem with the past, she thinks, is that there is no future in it. But wrong. She was wrong. This is where it leads the story never ends it is just reinvented. It's all true. Everything she tells you is a lie. You have to believe that. She's said this all before. She's read this in books about Windsor. She started writing in the margins of the books today but the notes stopped being about the history. They were just stories. Other stories and things found in the book not found in the book the problem she has is that she can't write everything together at once. Everything is now her primary interest. Now she is just changing the stories. She is in all of them. The problem with history is that there is no such thing. There is a spiral.

The spiral is not a hopeful shape. We say we spiral out of control. We say we spiral into disasters. We prefer arcs. A life plotted and executed. Rise. Peak. Decline. A death. We want to live in parabola rise crest fall like a wave. Water imagery and our love of narrative. But not true parabola. A happy ending. Any ending. Because even a bad ending is easy to tell. Here is what happened. Here is what went wrong. But the fall disgusts her. The arc. The spiral widens. It encompasses and yes, becomes harder to quantify, impossible to define an end to but it charts new ground, it upswings and renews it phoenixes out into the spaces beyond graphs. The arc dies. It fires up rocket-like and hangs desperate swingset trajectory and down. She wants to spiral outward. To collect more. A magnet among iron filings, an impossibility among facts. She sees this story moving.

It went like this. Carrie Nation was a Women's Temperance Movement member who died before Prohibition. She never got to see Canada and the States go officially dry. Her politicking and prayers fulfilled. Of course, Nation was known for taking a hatchet to bars and smashing stores of alcohol with large rocks while women from her church watched and sang hymns to the shocked onlookers and bar patrons shielding themselves from flying glass and hatchet. It is likely that the official policies would have been too relaxed for Nation. She called herself a bulldog running along at Jesus' feet and "Ravager" Misty Collins kept a framed photo of Nation over the bar in her speakeasy. The photo is unflattering and taken in the last years of Nation's life. She looks like a bulldog as much as anything, both in lack of grace and in utter self-possession and defiance. She brandishes her hatchet in the photo, which adds to the menacing effect somewhat. Misty admired Nation. Her willingness to struggle. Her ambition. Her violence and her arrest record. The fact that Jesus' bulldog would have tried to violently smash everything Misty had worked toward meant little to her. Most of the illegal patrons who visited her blind pig of a bar during the Canadian Prohibition years of 1918-1920 believed Misty displayed the picture of Nation ironically. Many raised jars of homemade liquor and illegally obtained beer to the bulldog in mocking toasts. But Misty's admiration for Nation was genuine. What Nation believed, Nation pursued. Without the right to vote, she struggled for power where she could find it. She spoke and handed out pamphlets against demon rum, she organized women's temperance groups, she pressured her husband and any politician who would listen to her to campaign against liquor. She protested saloons with her church groups. When that failed, she took up the hatchet. Nation, largely ignored because she was a woman, used her sex to aid her in the campaign. Even wielding an axe and destroying their livelihood, no gentleman saloon owner could raise a hand against her. Not with her entire church choir singing damnation at him. Men watched in impotent rage as Nation reduced their life's work to splinters, at a time when saloon keeping was perfectly legal. They would report her, the police would arrest her, but as the crime she was charged with was destruction of property and what amounted to little more than vandalism, Nation simply paid the fines and enjoyed her short stays in jail as a means of increasing her popularity and notoriety, often conducting sermonic interviews with newspapermen from her cell. Saloons famously began displaying signs that read "All Nations welcome but Carrie." It only made her more powerful. She gave temperance lectures and sold toy hatchets in front of the saloons. The proceeds went towards paying her arrest fees and producing more pamphlets. Nation realized that the bureaucracy and weak system that prevented the temperance force from achieving any kind of political victory over alcohol also protected her. For every saloon keeper who cursed her, a deacon would sing her praises. She was a woman, and her crimes, in the eyes of the law, were minor. There was only so much the system could do to stop her. From weakness, she found a frenetic, destructive strength.

"Ravager" Misty Collins had earned her nickname through attempting to live a life equal and opposite to the Bulldog. A woman of mixed-heritage and a widow by the age of 27, in 1915, Collins was living penniless and desperate in Essex County, Ontario, waiting tables and helping her cousins keep the books on their machine shop part-time. Collins worked tirelessly to achieve absolutely nothing at all. Then, in 1916, the State of Michigan declared Prohibition on alcohol and the Ravager found her own frenetic, destructive strength.

When Michigan went dry before the rest of America's Prohibition, enterprising smugglers began bringing in booze by the truckload, mostly from Chicago, where the breweries and distilleries were still going strong, despite increasing pressure from temperance and anti-liquor groups. But Michigan officials and church groups, which had been working to make Michigan dry since at least the 1850s, were ready for them. Roadblocks. Check stations. Men with guns. Many many men with guns. The profit to be made was humungous, but the risk was equally great. The initial smuggling rings began to scatter. Some were arrested, some killed. So Canadians began to simply pack up booze and bring it across the largely unpatrolled border. Men brought bottles in suitcases on the ferry. Women wore bottles strapped to their legs under their skirts and wore special corsets that strapped the booze to their waists. In 1916, the likelihood of these women being patted down or searched was slim. But this was small-time. The real money was to be made on the river. Boatloads of booze could be sent across at nearly any point along the Detroit River and Lake St. Clair. Everyone from Windsor to Stoney Point who lived on the water had a boat and a dock. Two decently sized islands situated directly between Detroit and Essex provided middle-ground opportunities. Much of the area was naturally reedy and marshy; hiding places were endless. When the river froze, jalopies could be driven across wherever the crossing was narrowest. Crates could be packed to float in case the cheap cars or boats sank. The merchandise could often be retrieved, even when the vehicle (and occasionally the driver) couldn't. There were police boats and spotters, but these were few and far between and unable to watch all of the riverfront. They were also notoriously easy to bribe. And the Ravager bribed them. Those who couldn't be bought woke to find their boats sunk or sinking. Holes shot through their floorboards and an empty whiskey bottle propped up in the cabin. The shotgun that blasted these boats was often fired by small, unassuming bookkeeper and waitress Misty Collins. Her tenacity and rampant destruction earned her the nickname "Ravager" before she was 30 years old.

Misty was largely apathetic, as far as her political agenda. While she believed in the growing struggle for the rights for women and blacks, she herself was never known to participate in any protests or activism. Her driving force appeared to be a belief in basic freedom, or at least a belief in profiting on those wanting to claim these freedoms. One of the only surviving quotes of this enterprising smuggler and secret tavern-owner is often related as: "If a man wants a drink, I say get him a drink. But make sure he can pay."

Collins, who worked as a server at a now-forgotten Walkerville area restaurant and tavern, kept the books for her cousins, the Berkler brothers, who acted as site managers at a small machine shop in the area. At the drying-up of Michigan, the Berklers saw the opportunity to make some money by allowing friends to use the machine shop, which was near the waterfront, as a staging ground for the packaging and loading of crates full of rum. The week leading up to the drop, the men involved brought only small amounts of whiskey and rum so as not to attract attention and hid it away in the Berkler's shop. On the night of the drop, the men assembled to begin packaging the liquor into crates and loading it into the Berklers' truck. As the night wore on, however, the men either became too inebriated on their own stock, or lost their nerve, and one by one either slunk out into the night or fell asleep. Misty, who had been balancing the books for the shop and listening with growing annoyance to the drunk men's plans, apparently finished packaging the materials by herself, drove the truck to the riverside, and helped the American smugglers waiting at the docks load the crates onto their boat by moonlight. The bemused men gave Misty an envelope filled with cash and a Detroit telephone number with which to arrange the next pickup. The next morning Misty gave the money to her cousins, but kept the telephone number. She told her cousins that she would be the one responsible for organizing any future operations, and that was that. Collins joined figures like Hilda Stone, known for driving trucks of booze into the Midwest by herself, and "Spanish Marie" Waits, queen of the Cuban operation smuggling into Florida, as one of the most important women of the rum-running trade. By all accounts, she didn't care about her infamy. She liked the money and she liked the lifestyle. She came to keep a picture of a woman who would have despised her over her bar and a sawed-off shotgun under it. Misty Collins did not give a fuck.

No maybe not like that. Keep it academic in tone? Or will this sort of writing set it apart from all the other projects? Focus more on the fact that she was half-black and most of the crew working for her was white? Imply that the Collins side of her family may be descended from Misty? But she's not black. Why is that the first thing she thought of? Would they expect her to be black if she stressed that, and, if so, would it then be disingenuous to stress that aspect?

Many believed Prohibition's true purpose was to keep liquor from blacks. White drinkers, who generally enjoyed greater social and economic influence, would still be able to get their fill through bootlegging and private production, while many blacks would not have the same options. The fact that the generalized racism of the time ensured that many whites received slaps on the wrist for bootlegging and flagrantly breaking Prohibition while blacks tended to be punished to the full extent of the law supports this belief, although it could also simply be incidental to larger issues of inequality.

And…what? Other than speculation, what can she do with this information? Is this the history that they want?

FACULTY OF ARTS
DEPARTMENT OF HISTORY

Leaf Houri
403-581-3213
lhouri@ubowriver.ca

aabcehecbaa,
aabcehecbaabcehecbaabcehecbaabcehecbaabcehecbaaabcehec-
baaabcehecbaabcehecbaabcehecbaabcehecba
112358,
53211

Dr. Leaf Houri,
Graduate Chair, Department of History,
University of Bow River

aabcehecbaa,
01123581321345589144233377610987159725844181676510946177112865746368750251213931964183178 11_

IAN

Hangover keeps pounding; it's almost noon. Luckily I'm in the basement most of the day today. Cool and dark and Vince doesn't chatter at me too much. On days we don't have bodies to collect or make up I'm mostly record keeping. Since Jarrington is terrified of computers and Young Jarrington is a moron, I've more or less officially become the IT guy. Which runs the gamut from maintaining records, the website, and updating whatever I can on the horribly out-of-date machines they keep in the funeral home. I'm amusing myself by looking through the search history on the computer in the downstairs office when Young Jarrington rings through from upstairs. I can see it's him but I'm supposed to answer with the company greeting so

    Jarrington Family Funeral Home, Ian speaking how can I

    "Your girlfriend is on line one," says a light female voice.

    Oh thanks, Jan.

    Jan Jarrington. Young Jarrington's oldest daughter. She's 16 and apparently watching the phones today, which means the Jarringtons Young and Old are selling. Or out. I remember that it will be summer break soon and that I'm in for Jan's mindless goading for months. At least she doesn't come into the back of house often. From down here we can't even hear the phones upstairs, and the soundproofing is useful when Vince drops an instrument. Or swears about what a fat bastard someone's dearly departed was.

"No problem, Crypt Keeper," Jan says. She is as big an idiot as her father. She will probably be my boss one day.

I figure Becky calling me at work is a very serious Oh Shit. The car was gone when I got home and I was a little drunk. Probably a little too drunk to have driven Jarrington's car home but well, I did. If she was gone I figured it was to blow off steam from being pissed at me being gone so late. But also I figured I dodged a bit of a bullet. I gargled and threw my clothes in the hamper, wanting to get the smell of beer off me. I didn't notice Athene wearing any perfume but I think I read somewhere that women have a better sense of smell than men. I wanted to shower but she could come in while I was in the shower or see that the shower had been used recently. That would make her assume the worst; she would assume that I was seeing another woman. Which I wasn't. Not really. I technically didn't do anything wrong, but I don't think there's any possible way I could explain going to drink with that young a girl as anything right. I got in bed and fell asleep before Becky got home. This morning she was in the bed next to me. Asleep and peaceful. No angry notes. No rage awakened by my morning work alarm. Set to the wrong time. She just rolled over and mumbled to me to have a nice day like she always does. I showered and dressed quickly and quietly, and left. Tripped over a pile of history books on my way out. She must be trying for school again. That will likely make for a depressing household soon. More depressing. I picked one of the books up and flipped musty pages. Rum-running. Smugglers. Flappers. Murders. More interesting than her usual fare and more relevant to her history thing than *The Jetsons*, I guess, but still not really anything I see much value in. Put the books back in a pile where she'd left them. Shut the door as softly as possible. Drove Jarrington's car to his funeral parlour. My guilty conscience faded behind my hangover. By the time I get home it will be forgotten or be a mild annoyance at best. That is the hope. But apparently she is calling me. She doesn't call very often and when she does I'm generally in Oh Shit territory. I press the button for line one and say hello, skipping the script patter.

"Hey. The girl who picked up said 'sure thing, Becky' when I asked to speak to you."

Athene.

Athene.

"Yes. Hello."

Well. A different Oh Shit. But still.

Hi. Why are you calling me? At work? I didn't give you this number.

Did I? I don't think I blacked out at all. I didn't drink *that* much.

"Is Becky your wife?"

What do I even say here.

Girlfriend. Is everything alright? Why are you calling?

"Funny, you didn't mention a girlfriend last night." She doesn't sound angry. More amused. Amused at my expense, specifically. At what she imagines to be my discomfort. I am rather discomforted. I think of what to say. You didn't ask? Well, you didn't talk about the other men you drink with? We didn't do anything it wasn't a date I didn't think I had to-

No. I didn't.

"Interesting."

Athene, look.

"Okay, I'll leave it alone. For now. Listen, are you burning anyone today?"

What? Cremations? No. We don't have any cremations scheduled.

"So that means you're done at five, right?"

What the hell is this?

Yeah. I mean, probably. Unless Jarrington needs something done or. Or something happens.

"If someone dies."

Yes.

"What a life you lead. Waiting on the dead. Like Hel."

What?

What? Like hell?

"Nevermind. Can you pick me up at five? Or as close to that as you can?"

What? No. Why?

"There's something I want to show you. And you can see where I work if you want. It's neat. Because you had fun last night."

I did.

I did?

"You did. I just really think you'll get a kick out of this place and I'd like to finish our conversation. It's just that. Well, talking to you helps me work through some things. Look, just do this and I'll leave you alone after that if that's what you want."

Is that what I want? I behaved myself, but from what I remember of my beer twisted dreams, I fucked the living hell out of her in my mind last night. Those hazel eyes. And gasping. Her smallness beneath the weight of my body. What the hell is wrong with me? I almost say yes. But there is no way I can come home late from work two nights in a row. I have to make peace with Becky. Take the uncomfortable domestic silence I've earned.

Jesus. Okay, but it can't be tonight. Do you work tomorrow?

"No, I'm part-time. I work again on Friday."

Okay. I'll pick you up at five on Friday.

"Unless you have to burn someone."

Well, right. But as close to five as possible.

"Alright."

Okay. Hey, wait. Where am I going? Where do you work?

"The Bird of Prey Centre. Just outside town, you know it?"

Bird of… you aren't going to, like, make me watch you feed mice to hawks or something?

"What? No. Jesus Christ, Ian. I work in the gift shop."

Oh.

"I'm a cashier, asshole. I have nothing to do with the birds."

Sorry, I just. You are kind of. I don't know, that malice thing of yours.

"Half of that was to scare you."

Well it worked. I was half convinced you were some creepy little pixie girl murder thing.

"Nice."

Sorry.

"Front gate at five on Friday."

So what is it you want to show me, then?

"Five on Friday. I'll be waiting. Like Hel."

That's twice you said that. What is that? Hell? Hell waits?

"She does. But you're probably thinking of the wrong thing. It's Norse mythology, don't worry about it. I'm just being a creepy pixie."

And she hangs up on me. The Bird of Prey Centre and Norse myths. Jesus. I get that she's a smart, troubled kid, or whatever, and she's attractive enough that I'm sure she gets indulged, but her whole life *is* an indulgence and now I'm indulging her, too. I'm having trouble remembering that she *is* a kid. Not some spirit. Not a ghost from my past. And I'm indulging her. Those eyes. And yes, fine. Those tits. Foot bumping my leg under the table. Flesh through fabric in dim light. No. Indulge this and be free of her. I have to think of some excuse to tell Becky for Friday. For why I'll be home late again. Will smooth things over tonight first. Vince calls for my help from the chemical storage closet and I click closed his search history on the computer to go help him. We're all just monsters down here. I should make fun of him for that. A nerd knows better, he should be clearing his search history. Unless Young Jarrington specifically uses the computer down here for. Ugh. Hell. I'll look into these myths later if I get a chance. A good chance she's not really creepy and just doing well on her mythology unit in Social Studies or History or Creative Writing or whatever.

BECKY

Becky takes the money Ian kept stashed in his gym bag and buys rum with it. Spiced rum and dark rum. Rum named for fictional people and monsters. She's not sure, in the moment, if she's being impulsive, mean spirited, or defiant. She is sure that she wants to get profoundly pirate drunk. Ian cancelled his gym membership seven months ago. Had not gone for two months before that. Taking the money stale with his scent is a punishment, perhaps. Or now she is justifying. Were they common-law, technically? How long had they lived together now? What was hers was his, why shouldn't she? Of course, nothing is hers. She feels she has nothing anymore. She is nothing. Bullshit. She is a pirate.

After being asked to leave the library by a different librarian than the one who had initially spoken to her, Becky finds herself in a moment of panic. Despite reading for hours, she has barely made a dent in the history books she has gathered. She can't check the books out. She doesn't have her student card. No, she thinks. Almost right. I am not a student here. My student card does not exist. Becky gathers the books, already she thinks of them as *her* books. Even stuffing her messenger bag to capacity (strap biting shoulder; seams threatening) she has a cumbersome armload. She feels small and murderous. Weighed down, but potentially powerful. She can't go back to

Coaldale without the research. And she won't be able to come back to the school again without borrowing Ian's car. And gas money. The need to borrow has suddenly repulsed her. She is aware of the irony of this realization coming to her in a library. She is aware of the impatient librarians eyeing her and waiting for her to shuffle her ponderousness out so that they can lock up and go home. She is aware of pain in her left wrist, the one she had broken as a girl, beneath the weight of river thieves and rum-runners. Of the sharp corner of a book poking rib. Of the obnoxious perfume the rude librarian is wearing. Borrowing. No. Her plan is simple; she is going to walk through the security arches until they started beeping, and then run. Weighed down and only somewhat familiar with the campus layout in the daylight, Becky is fairly confident that in the darkness she will not be able to make it to her car before security is called. In her fevered moment, she doesn't care. As she walks past the front desk and begins to steel herself for her run, Becky sees one of the librarians grab an armload of books off the desk.

"Tommy," the girl calls to some unseen person. "Switch off the arches, would you? I already logged out the system." Tommy has apparently flipped a switch or input a code or done a rain dance, and the librarian, the one who had been terse with Becky, and Becky passed through the security arches together without checking out their books. As Becky turns and walks in the general direction of her car, the girl calls out a fairly sarcastic wish that Becky have a great night. It's a small piracy, she realizes, but Becky is energized by her tiny crimes. She considers speeding down the highway back towards Coaldale. Racing anyone she pulls up next to. Flipping off or flashing truckers. She does none of these things. She stops at STOPNEAT, an all-night diner that looks promisingly like a greasy spoon from the parking lot but is disappointingly clean and without character inside. She makes small talk with the old man running the place, and drinks coffee while drinking in her books. She cannot bring herself to go home. Becky is disappointed that the old man doesn't ask her any questions about herself. She wanted to invent a story. Fabricate an identity with its own history and excitement and romance. He just pours coffee. Hums along to the radio. Becky doesn't even get to the frantic lies. Pressured and on the spot. Wait I thought you said you were an heiress. No no I meant travelling inventor. She wants to be caught in a lie or be suspected. The old man leaves her alone. The only other customers are truckers wanting coffee and a break. Becky doesn't want to tell them a story; she's afraid the story they would tell back would be better thought out. She has to go about inventing history. She needs more time for research and preparation.

It's late when she pulls into her/Ian's driveway. Jarrington's black sedan already there. She feels guilt for her temporary abandonment. For her temporary theft of books. For the resentment and venom that has more and more shaped the way she thinks about the man she shares her life with.

Inside, Ian is asleep. Becky closes the bedroom door softly. She does not want to go to bed. She wants to pore over her booty. She wants to drink more coffee but is afraid the smell will wake Ian. Instead she cracks a can of Coke—wincing at the bark of the aluminum top snapping—and sits on the floor amidst her books. Inventing.

When the clocks in the sitting room say that Ian will be getting up in two hours, Becky piles her books and climbs into the bed next to him. Pretends to sleep. Plays possum during his alarm, ablutions, and egress. Feigns a half-asleep "have a good day" while nervously awaiting his absence. Becky slips back out of bed as she hears the front door close. She remembered the money in the gym bag as she lay waiting for him to leave her to her imagined histories. She'll take the money and buy rum, she thinks. She'll take the rum and she'll write history. First coffee, then reading, then rum. This was an itinerary and arc.

Out towards Tecumseh, fields and houses on the water. Small mostly, shaped by wind, near water but already some mansions cropping up. Automobile money or smuggler barons, new money moving outwards from the city. Windsor growing as Detroit gets bigger, Windsor growing as Detroit gets thirstier. Out from river toward the lake, not as much out here yet. Shacks, boathouses, lots of liquor. Away from the smog and lights of the city I expect the moon to be brighter, to jump out threatening and put too much light on the water, but cloudy tonight and the few stars that peek through seem muted.

Guy out here supplying for us tonight is Babe's friend. Babe says he's an idiot but an alright idiot. He's got a boatload for us cheap so we'll take it and he can be whatever kind of idiot he wants. Babe owns the Chappell house in Sandwich, but he's got his hands in most of the smaller operations out here in one way or another. Out here near the shores there are a number of tunnels from sheds and houses that go right up to the water. Some are holdovers from fighting or trading with Indians or from the War of 1812 when supplies needed to fight the Americans were run up to fort Windsor from every conceivable direction. Weapons caches, ammunition dumps, hiding places. Some are supposed to be part of the Underground Railroad. Other traps and tunnels are new. Some my cousins and I have helped dig. Babe's friend, Leroy is his name, Leroy has a house and a blind pig by the water here and I guess a tunnel under one or both of them. Buildings up on the bank. Tunnels should lead out somewhere around here. We cut engine and drift in. Paddle slowly and quiet, looking for landmarks and signs. A kid, probably thirteen, a shadow in a cap, appears on the shore from behind dark trees. Lights a small lamp and flashes it. Twice. Twice more. Once. He walks away from the trees and down a bank onto the beach. We guide the boat in towards his light on the beach. As we drag the boat up men come from nowhere. From a hole hidden in the bank or a trapdoor under the sand. This kind of trap door smuggling is what made Caribbean pirates their fortunes. Also got a lot of them killed. We have guns but Leroy's men don't. Or don't have them in plain sight. Some look nervous. Big men sweating hauling casks and barrels up from some awful spidertrap and finding us with guns on their beach. There is style in what we do.

I put up my gun, give it over to Jim and start helping load barrels. Direct the others and heft. Leroy emerges from the dark wherever of the spiderhole. It's in the bank after all, just a passage cut amongst the rocks and sandy loam. They have what look like small pans driven into the walls and little candles gutter every so often. There is style. Leroy shakes my hand. Chatters about the night. The water. He's carrying nothing himself. Breath reeks of rum. He talks too damn loud. I respect a man who has no fear but I start wondering if he has no sense as he bellows on. Spraklin, that loudmouthed idiot, the so-called fighting parson, who preaches temperance with his gunbelt on and splinters the pulpit under his fist as he denounces me and my kind, he might be a joke, but he and his men are a joke that carry guns. And they patrol. And despite being deputized, half of them are no better than bloodthirsty thugs looking for an excuse to squeeze a gun off at someone. Most are ex-convicts. Most crazy as all shit. I hush my boys down hoping Leroy and his men will take the hint. He comes to himself suddenly. Realizes he is on a beach filled with illegal booze and armed smugglers. Realizes how easy it would be to get shot. He growls at his men to shut the fuck up. As I work I realize they all reek, not just Leroy. At least one is stumbling. Sons of bitches. Roaring drunk with my merchandise and armed lunatics behind every shadow. If a drop of what was promised me is missing I'll want to shoot these bastards myself. But Jim runs a quick count and everything looks good. He smacks all of the barrels to hear inside. Leroy wouldn't cross Babe—he's got too much influence right now and he's a good person to know when you're in trouble—but he's also drunk and apparently an idiot. Never too careful. These men need shooting, but no one gets shot tonight.

But people did get shot. The most famous incident occurred when J.L. Spraklin, the fighting parson, shot Babe Trumble to death at Trumble's bar, the Chappell house. They had known each other from boyhood. Had never been friends. When Spraklin was appointed special Director of Prohibition the relationship became openly antagonistic. There were many purveyors or suspected purveyors of demon rum, but Spraklin targeted Trumble. Trumble accused Spraklin of harassment, disrupting his legal businesses with charges he couldn't prove. Spraklin's house was shot up and the minister put the blame on Trumble. He took to wearing his gun at all times. His gunbelt clearly visible while he preached. Finally the fighting parson went into the Chappell house in the early hours of November 6, 1920. Went in and shot the man to death in front of his wife and friends. Spraklin was arrested and charged but said it was self defense. Trumble went for his gun, Spraklin said. His word against the wife of a bootlegger's. He was released. These things we know. These things are in the books. Names and dates and charges and deaths. Material records and stories that swirl around them where the two intertwine. Witnesses scattered like seed to wind. Misty was one of the friends thought to have been there to see Trumble killed, but no one knows for sure. She never came forward, if so. Her word might not have been believed and she would have implicated herself in smuggling, liquor production, possession, racketeering, and anything else Spraklin and his bunch wanted to throw at her. If Misty admired The Bulldog's tenacity, she had no mind to emulate her jail time. If Misty was even there. She might have been home, asleep. Or in her own bar. Or making love in the squeak of a jalopy parked by the whiskey river. Not anything is possible; we believe some things must remain. Or it spirals. That line falls where? If Ravager Misty had blasted a man's head off on a beach, would we know about it? If there is no story, there is no history. What histories has Ian buried or cremated without a story? What histories does he murder? She needs to know more. There are libraries to rob. There are stories to plunder.

IAN

Friday. Watching the sales office upstairs for the rest of the day. Manning the till. Holding down the fort. Doing some third cliché about working. I'm not great at coming up with things. I'm very bored. The people who call don't seem to be alive. Disembodied voices. Jarringtons Old, Young, and Pubescent gone out. Vince in the basement among the transfers and chemicals. Blissfully immune to customers, phone calls, conversations. I have Jarrington's memos taped next to the phone for dealing with inquiries and environmentalists. I have price sheets and sales patter memorized. I know when to wait and nod. To let grief express itself and pick the best moment to sell. I recognize weak links. People assume women are more emotional than men, that they are preyed upon by funeral directors. It's true they are more likely to cry in the showroom. When I show them a receptacle or a casket they are more likely to say it out loud. "It's what he would have wanted" and then tears. But tears don't spend and men are the real soft touches. Especially when it's their mothers who have passed. They are so desperate to avoid the unmanly tears. The sadness and reality of the situation. They want so very much to pretend that this is just another business transaction and that they are mastering their way through it. Wallets fly out. Chequebooks appear. They shake your hand and grit their teeth and thank you for being so professional like they are surprised by it. This is our profession. We fleece their grief. This business is the domain of monsters. We are merciful compared to the big houses. They will burn your loved ones down and put ashes inside tacky jewellery. Charge a premium for music at the remembrance service held in the parlour. Speaking fees for a eulogy when the eldest son gets too choked up to speak. Some will present something that would be better suited to entombing a Pharaoh before they are finished. We will try to sell your mother into the Monarch line, true, but at least that's the worst we do. At least until Old Jarrington goes. He's a cheap old bastard, but he has some standards. He's on record as wanting to be left out for crows and dogs when he dies. Young Jarrington, of course, will use his father's death as a business opportunity. And honestly, he'd be stupid not to. Old Jarrington is well liked in the community. The funeral home proprietor will end up in a well publicized wake displayed serenely (Vince and I do good work even when we're hungover and phoning it in; we will bust our asses on the old man) in a top-of-the-line Monarch. The people will say he looks just like he's sleeping. He looks peaceful. Someone will say he looks better now than he did when he was—and someone will shush him or cough. Laugh quietly or shuffle feet. Young Jarrington will wipe away a fake tear and deliver a mostly plagiarized but still touching eulogy about family and continuance. He'll be reluctant in his assumption of his father's duties. He won't move his things into his father's office for at least three days. His daughter will be named sales manager and head of funeral direction shortly thereafter. Her things will be moved into this office and it will never be mine. Maybe Vince will die or become so engrossed in a Dungeons and Dragons game he'll just disappear. But most likely not. The phone rings and another noisy transfer asks for pricing information. I look at the time on the wall clock and for a moment forget that it is the right time. Begin to do math to understand where in time I am before I realize it's futile. Two hours until I pick up Athene.

I'm back downstairs sweeping up and getting ready to close up when Becky calls. This time it is actually her. Guilt swims through my system like disease. She knows. Knows that I haven't done anything. I've wanted to. She knows.

"Hey, Ian, how's the day? Almost done?"

Yeah almost. Uh, it was okay. Slow. I was upstairs most of the day.

"Doing sales?"

Well, no actual sales. We didn't have any bereaved in today. But answering calls.

"Well, still, that's experience, right? Like for when you are done training. When you are an actual funeral director."

If I am ever done. She doesn't sound angry. She sounds encouraging. Maybe condescending. An actual funeral director. She is asking questions politely because she does not care about my job. But does not sound angry. So that is a win.

I guess.

"Listen, you're out tonight, aren't you? Or late or something?"

She wasn't even paying attention when I lied to her. Told her I'll be out with Vince again. Was going to try to be social and play games with his friends. A specific enough lie but not so detailed that I can't remember it. I'm scum.

Uh. Yeah. Late.

"Okay, sure. You should eat while you're out, then. I'm going to be gone a while tonight too, so you're fending for yourself."

Jesus. Why am I getting away with this? Why is this so easy?

Oh. Okay sure.

Do I ask her where she's going? Do I have a right to? It might be dangerous to set a precedent of a lot of questions being asked. Athene is 17. Scum.

"I'm going to go in on this research project. I'll have the car"

My car.

"at the school tonight"

What school?

"so you'll have to take one of Jarrington's cars around, okay? Or get a ride with Vince?"

She's not asking my permission, she's just informing me. I go from terrified to indignant and then get a hold of myself.

Yeah, uh, no problem. Have fun?

"Ha. I'm not sure if research is *fun*, but thanks."

We hang up and I check the clock. Athene. Waiting for me by the wounded eagle enclosure. The marshland vegetation exhibits. I googled the hell out of the Bird of Prey Centre while I was bored upstairs. Waiting like Hel. Oh, shit. I forgot to look that up. I'm halfway through the parking lot as I realize it. I pull out my cell and call Becky. The guilt now vague and blunted.

"Hey again."

Hey.

Do I pause? I feel like I pause before I say

honey. Hey, this is weird, but do you know anything about Norse mythology?

"Norse?"

Yeah. Like Thor.

"Yeah, no. I know what it is. Just surprising. A bit, yeah. I did a course on Scandinavian history in undergrad."

No, not history. More like the myths.

"Well. There is a certain amount of overlap. Why do you ask?"

Just. Something I overheard. At the parlour. Vince is kind of a nerd for that stuff. Do you know who Hel was? Not like hell the place, I mean. I think it's a woman.

"Sure. She was a goddess. Well, sort of. She ruled the Norse version of the underworld. Which basically was like hell the place."

Like with fire and the devil?

"Not exactly. But eternal damnation, anyway. Standard underworld mythology stuff. That was her punishment."

What was she punished for?

"Well, for being born, I guess. She was Loki's daughter."

The same Loki from the Thor comics?

"Um. I imagine so. Comics are more your area of research. He's in everything because in their history, he plays an important role."

You said history again. But, it's mythology you're talking about, though, right? Stories?

"Everything is storytelling."

Okay. But there wasn't an actual Loki, right?

"I'm ignoring that question. Anyway, Loki had children. Different sets of children depending on the source of the myth."

Source?

"The different versions of the *eddica* and the runes and stones."

I am extremely unsure of what any of that means.

"Don't worry about it. The important thing, for the sake of me telling you this story, is what happened to Loki's children."

Okay. So, what happened?

"They were punished."

What did they do wrong?

"They were born of Loki. I guess that was bad enough. Well, one was a giant serpent that was fated to kill Thor and one was a giant wolf that would eat the sun. Or wait that might have been another wolf. There are a lot of wolves in those myths, is the thing."

So what was Hel?

"Actually I don't think she's really described. She was just a girl. Which doesn't sound as bad as a Thor-killing serpent or Sun-eating wolf. Or no wait. The wolf kills Odin, I think."

Does Hel kill anyone?

"I don't think so. But maybe being a girl was bad enough. Or I guess the whole Loki-spawn thing. Anyway, they tied the wolf up, they threw the serpent in the sea, but Hel they banished to an entirely different realm."

So Hel, the woman or goddess or whatever. Would she collect the damned? Did she go and collect the dead? Like did she have to go and get them, or did they get banished to this place too, or what?

"Where did this come from?"

Just. Just something... Vince said. About us being like her. We collect the dead. The transfers.

"Oh. Sort of. But the people who went to the underworld in Norse myth were cowards or oath breakers. Those who died bravely went somewhere else. Like a warrior's heaven."

Warrior heaven.

"Yeah. They sat around and drank beer and boasted about their great deeds to each other. And they had big-titted woman warrior angels that brought them there."

No shit.

It is possibly good that I didn't look this up on a sales computer.

"The Vikings were kind of weird."

Right. So. The comparison doesn't really work, then. I mean, unless we only picked up bad people. Oath breakers. Or were... warrior angels?

"Big-titted ones, yes. And I mean, it does kind of. Not Valhalla, but I mean Hel. Most of the people you transfer are elderly and die in their beds, don't they? Or their homes. They waste away."

Yeah. Most. Waste is a good word for it. Most are almost kind of shrivelled by the—

"Yuck. Stop. Okay, so that's the straw death. They didn't die bravely, so they wasted away into old age. To the Vikings, that was cowardice. Those people would go to Hel. In Hell."

That's pretty harsh.

"Well. They were Vikings. They were pretty good at harsh. Oh! I remembered something cool. A ship built of their fingernails will carry all the damned back to the world when the end comes. Ragnarok. I think Hel is in charge of that."

A ship.

"Yes."

Made of dead men's fingernails.

"Right? Vikings were pretty messed up."

Are you just making this up now?

"Well, I mean, it's myth. But people believed it. Oh, man.

I haven't thought about any of this stuff in years. I need to look this stuff up after I'm done with the Ravager."

The what?

"Oh. Just a. It's not important. It's just another story I'm working on."

Oh. Oh your research, okay.

"Is that… Did you just want to ask about Vikings?"

What? Oh. Yeah. Well, and I mean, to tell you to drive safe. Don't stay at the library too late.

"Ah, are you worried about me?"

Well. And my car.

Of course I am.

"You're sweet sometimes."

We hang up. I start the car. The black sedan sliding out towards the outskirts of this outskirt town. Towards Athene. I'm sweet.

I know the street she's taking us down. Where it happened. But the house isn't even there anymore. It's a church now. But I'll let this play out. She hums quietly along to my radio. I like the smell of her in my car. Jarrington's car. We use the vans to haul bodies, the cars for transporting the bereaved or supplies to funeral grounds. Never had a girl in the front seat humming before. Cut-off shorts and flip-flops. Her legs pale. Hint of freckle to her skin. I tell myself to keep my eyes on the road. Scrapes on long shin.

I've been at burials for Jarrington in the little graveyard they made when the church bought out the property down here. Three years ago they put this up? Something like that.

"It's a church now," she says. Matter-of-factly.

Yeah, I. I thought maybe you didn't know. Didn't want to say anything.

"So you would have just driven me to see a house that isn't there?" She sounds amused.

I guess.

"I'm not sure if that is sweet or not." She smiles, though. Eyes. Road. It's not sweet. It's creepy. Why am I here? Because if I do this, I can put her out of my mind. Give her whatever closure she needs and go back to my life. Be done with this. Yes. That is what I want. Her toenails chipped plum. Long fine bones of toe and ankle.

"No, I know. I come here sometimes," she says absently. We roll slowly under trees and she watches the shadow of overhang through the window. Looks like she is counting individual leaves. I nearly hit a parked car and tell myself to watch the fucking road.

She points and I pull into a small lot. Gravel crunches below and she smells like candy. Like the perfume and lip balm of a 17-year-old.

We get out of the car and walk around the church. Down a small white path and through a gate. Among headstones and crosses.

"Here," she says.

Nadine Daniels. 1972-2006. Taken before her time.

That's impossible.

"It's my mother."

No, I mean. This was still your. This was a house. Or houses. I don't know where the property ended. This graveyard didn't exist when. In 2006.

"I know that. It's just a headstone. My uncle and aunt did it. They sold the land to the church. They gave money. Helped build it. They go to this church, which is kind of weird to me. They asked me to Christmas service here this year."

They put a marker for your mother in when they helped build the church?

"Yes."

I recognize the stonework. Frank or his family in Lethbridge. He does shitty work and the monument is looking ancient after only... What? Is it three years? I don't remember when the church went up. I don't know the groundskeeper here very well. He doesn't work too hard by the looks of the grounds. I wonder if other people would even notice.

It's uh. It's nice. I mean it's nice that they did that.

"Yeah, I guess. I mean, it's nice that they care about her. Cared. I come here sometimes. I don't know where they really buried her."

There wasn't a funeral?

I search my memory for anything connected to my first removal. Did we do the arrangements after the transfer? Usually that's how it goes. Obviously they didn't have me doing any of the funeral directing when I was still just starting to transfer, but you'd think I'd remember more about the first. I don't. I don't remember.

"When she died. After it happened, my aunt took me to stay in B.C. for a little while. With my grandma. But she died too and my aunt and me... Well. We came back here, to my uncle's house. But I didn't stay with them."

Why not?

She shakes her head. We stand before her mother's stone. I find myself wondering if Athene has her own place. If she doesn't live with her family, does she live in foster care? Or alone? Maybe with a roommate. Even in this moment the reptile opportunist part of my brain is considering the possibility that there exists a place where I could have sex with this girl. It's not a conscious plan or desire. Just a thought that happens somewhere in the worst part of my mind. I want to attribute this to being male more than to being evil. But maybe I'm forgiving a lot in myself.

"When I. This is stupid, but when I got my U of C acceptance and my scholarship and everything, I brought the letters down here. I rode my bike and read the 'we are pleased to inform you' letters to the stone. Like I was showing her what I'd done."

She stops. Voice low but not thick. Slight wind and her hair sways slightly but no tears. I am such a fucking scumbag. She laughs.

"The layers of stupid to that. Like, not just that she's not alive, she's also not even buried here. I know it's ridiculous but still."

Well. It comforts you. Or whatever.

Or whatever. I will never make funeral director. Keep me away from the bereaved, Jarringtons.

"It does, yeah." She looks at me. "They won't tell me where she's really buried, Ian."

Plaintive.

"My uncle and aunt. They won't say. They don't talk about it. I. I need to know."

Oh. Oh I see. I can. You want me to.

She looks away, something like embarrassed. Looks back at her mother's stone. Taken before her time. Taken where?

Yeah. Okay. I'll look it up. I'll pull the files on the. On your mother's arrangements.

Of course I will. Of course she wanted something from me. I feel stupid. Old and fat. Just look at her.

Happy to help.

Something in the way I say this betrays me. She looks at me again. Head tilted up at my greater height. Eyes squinted as the sun begins to dip. Or squinting as she gauges weakness? She is a predator. She told me. Or she is a young girl who wants help?

"Ian, look-"

No. No, it's fine. Yeah, no I mean it. I'm happy to help. I'll see whatever I can dig up.

Dig up. Jesus Christ. But she does not wince. She says nothing else. Nods once slowly. Brushes hair behind her ear. Of course she does. We stand here a while longer. I thought. I don't know what I thought. I thought this was going somewhere. Maybe I was afraid this was going somewhere. I don't go anywhere. We get back in the car. I drive.

Have you ever been to see your dad?

"Go and visit him in prison, you mean? "

Yeah.

"No. Never had an interest."

Really?

"I wouldn't know what to say. I don't know if there is anything to say. If there's a point to saying anything."

Yeah. I get that. Sorry, that was maybe a stupid question.

"No, it's fine. But, what about you? What are your parents like?"

Oh. My dad worked in the auto industry. He retired a couple of years ago. And mom—

"What they do. What they are. Those are just tiny eulogies. What are they *like*?"

Oh.

"Do you do that? For your job, I mean. Write little eulogies to summarize people's lives?"

Sometimes a funeral director puts a little something together, yeah. If the family doesn't want to or can't.

"But you aren't a funeral director."

Well. In training.

"Training. Transferring. To what? For what? You fascinate me."

Okay.

"You tell these little stories but yours goes nowhere. Willfully."

Now you're just being shitty.

"Ha. You're right. Turn up here."

There's nothing down there. Farms for miles.

"I know, just turn. Now keep driving."

I drive the car. Field after field. Road hypnosis and wishful thinking and I can just see it. She would lean over. Tuck hair behind ear and pull me out. I would say what are you doing like I don't know and she would say just don't crash the fucking car and

"The service road up there. If you go right you can get back to the main road. You know where Elmtree is?"

Yes I do. Do I feign ignorance? Try to get us lost. She clearly knows where we are. That would be shitty of me. Hope sparks in my lizard sexdrive brain. Does she want me to know where to go so she doesn't have to navigate? So she can. I should encourage—how do I encourage this? I used to date. I used to drive girls around in my car. I drove Becky around. I feel like what happens now is I put my hand on her knee. It is entirely possible that that is not what happens now but

BECKY

There must be arc to it. *She* knows that it is a spiral and the spiral is one of many within a hydra but there *is* the desire to tell stories. Or to hear them, in this case. Dear Miss Burgess, we regret to inform you that we are interested in the type of history that fits a storybook. Fits a dissertation. Looking to the margins to find stories, newness, interest. The more important she can make an obscure historical person seem, the better. They have to have a *story*. Misty didn't just live a life and die and rot. Entropy and reduction to basic compounds. Children carry genes, people she interacted with carrying on, compounds feeding worms. No. Her story ended. She was a woman of colour and she killed men. Or she saw them killed. Or. There needs to be more arc to it. Becky needs to learn arc. She knows spiral can be traced she knows the math but this is not a story. Assuming zero value to begin we go one and then one again and thereafter marry the last two. Simple summation gives us the curve. Not arc, not even individual spirals but really a mad arrangement of spirals interacting and branching; genesis and termination everywhere. To look at any one section any individual turning and call it arc is to look upon the many-headed hydra and fear one fang only. But she is tasked. What is the arc within the hydra? It is lying. The part she breaks off and shows them. A new line she draws on the graph without any actual values. Simply an attractive shape. Yes. And sell that. Stare at anything long enough and you will see patterns in it. She will simply help the eye along. She will provide the first two values and suggest their sum.

Ravager Misty had something of a knack for staying one step ahead of authorities. Whenever possible, she seemed to keep her operations as legal as she could. She and her cousins were among the first to begin shipping booze across the Detroit River in what are now known infamously as "Cuba Runs." When the rest of the United States looked to follow in Michigan's footsteps by threatening to go dry under the Volstead Act, both Berkler brothers applied for boating licences. Handwriting samples from the Berkler accounts books and several of their delivery bills have survived to the present day; while it is difficult to be certain if it was Misty who applied and wrote tests in her cousins' names, both licences were applied for in the same hand, and a hand that matches neither of the Berklers' crude writing styles. By the time America went dry, the Berklers had embarked upon the legal exportation of spirits to Cuba. The fact that the same Berkler boats made the run from Windsor to "Cuba" sometimes four or five times in a single day seemed to elude authorities, who could only check for boat licences, export permits, and approved destinations. Since it was legal to export liquor to Cuba, there was little authorities could do. Completely legal boat licence applications increased exponentially shortly before the Volstead act went into effect in the States. Part of the reason it was so difficult to stop the rum-running was that the smugglers were organized and, except for the act of smuggling itself, tended to do everything above board. The drop-offs happened in secret and the paperwork was forged well enough to appear to be in order. Twice investigators took a special interest in the Berklers and in Misty's plans and attempted more than the cursory checks Misty so easily sidestepped. One official quickly decided that a full investigation wasn't warranted and began driving a new car. The other proved obstinate. His investigation went on for some three months before he became one of the numerous unexplained Prohibition-Era disappearances. This interference was rare, though. There was simply too much smuggling, with not enough manpower to stop it. Misty and the Berklers were one among hundreds of operations moving booze across the river. Often the smuggling was small-time. Even zealous officials and police were hesitant to risk getting shot for what amounted to a few hundred dollars' worth of booze. But some, like Misty, had grander plans. She partnered with Babe Trumble and began using his Chappel House as a base and staging ground. Money poured in. The Berklers took to wearing furs. Misty was never ostentatious but at the height of her infamy, even she indulged. A photograph existed (unfortunately since my research started the collection the photograph was contained in was moved and a librarian mistakenly discarded the photograph and several others) that showed Misty and Trumble toasting one another. Trumble in a smart suit, a cane and new Trilby on the table between them. Misty, gloved, has a fine chain trailing from the wrist offering the toast to Trumble. The photo was black and white but the chain and the matching one around her neck were presumably gold. Her curls peeking from beneath a new Cloche hat look carefully coiffed. Of the gentlemen in the background of the photo, one has been identified as Charles, the eldest Berkler brother. He is talking to someone out of frame and has the slackened face of the carelessly drunk. The collar of his new fur crushed on one side, as if he'd fallen asleep on it. The only other clear face in the background belongs to a gentleman who has never been identified, but the cut of his suit and hat indicate that he too had money to throw around. The man's hand is on Charles' shoulder, apparently trying to attract his attention. Yet the man's face is turned towards the Ravager in the foreground. One wonders if, in trying to communicate something to the drunk Berkler, the man had suddenly been surprised to see a woman drinking among them. Or perhaps Misty had said something that had caught his attention. Was, perhaps, the man interested in Misty, and hoping Charles would introduce them? There is, or rather was, surely a story in the photograph, but it has been lost to

No. Always leave 'em wanting more can't work here. This is not the spiral. Risky enough to start this arc, can't invite others to look for it. Story and end and direction and answers. Impossible, simplified, stupid fucking answers.

Dear
Miss
Burgess
We regret
To inform you that

Sums and sequences everything

IAN

Nothing happened because nothing ever happens. We barely even speak except for her directing me to her friend's house. They are going to study together. Here. No straight here. The next left. This one. With the grey car. I still don't know what her living situation is. Going to study together. A high school girl. Jesus Christ. I can't go home. I drive around aimlessly and find myself pulling into the lot at Jarrington's. The black sedan ticks and cools next to the vans. The small golden "J" in script on their doors. Emblazoned on the glass. On the cards in my wallet above my name and my title. My title that ends in "in training" and has for years. Training. Transferring. Towards what? she had asked. And then. I unlock the side door to the building and let myself in. A trainee with a key. Because I'm a trainee who does everything. I answer the phones, I mop up, I collect and prepare the dead for their transition. The ceremony that acts as euphemism for the actual transition. The moment not so much between breath and silence as between muscle control and sphincter release. A trainee who could be a director by now at a corporate funeral home. Who would probably run this place if I were a Jarrington. What was I thinking?

    I punch in the code to the security system and shuffle towards the narrow staircase that leads to the basement. The bleach and scrub smell that rises from below. The mask and euphemism. I flick lights on absently as I pass. Some I don't. I would know my way around this basement with my eyes closed, now. I open the prep room and am hit with its cool air. The lights hum to life above me. The molecules in mercury vapour gradually exciting. The roller grumbles out and I'm looking at the remains of the kid who hanged himself. Now pumped full of chemicals and partially dressed. We will finish his prep tomorrow shortly before the funeral. Set him and spray him and tape him and tack him into place. Not surprisingly, you try not to have the finished product sitting for too long. It all goes to hell quickly. Finish setting them right before the viewing and hope their eyes don't pop open while their tearful family hovers over them for their last goodbye.

I fish a glove out of one of the omnipresent boxes of disposable latex on the instrument tables. Sheathe and press my thumb to his eyeball. Gently but not reverently. I palpate a small circle and feel what seems to be tiny grains of rice beneath the eyelid. This is actually a hard contact lens that has been scored outwards so that the jagged edges catch and keep the eyelid in place until rigor takes over. It's these plastic spikes of scoring I feel. I'm surprised Vince didn't use glue for this one. The contacts aren't perfect. They do pop sometimes. It's rare, sure, but with a kid, and a kid who died the way he did, there is probably going to be an extended viewing. People will want to see. To be there and ask questions silently of the body. Why, probably. Like they will be answered. Respect for the dead, for the family, for the suspension of the rules of the real world within the parlour will keep the talking urge from overpowering their silence. They will hold their peace until they file out. Shake hands and revert to the need. The predictable lead. I'm just so sorry. There are no words. If you need anything, *anything*. Hands pressed. Mothballed suits the worst smell in the room because Vince does good work. He will lie there, nearly smiling, while they work through grief and script. Hopefully he doesn't look to see who is talking about him. I make sure the lid is secure and step back. What are you now? No longer transferring. That nothing word that means. No. Just meat. Heavy quiet meat.

She's seventeen, I tell him. He says nothing.

Why in the hell. I mean. I don't even know if I want that.

He remains uninterested in my need.

I wanted that. I want her now. Warmth.

And what if. I mean, I didn't fuck her. I mean. I didn't do anything. But if she had wanted to get lost on the backroads and hadn't just wanted a ride to her friend's house, would I have done something? It's not impossible that I would have. But I don't know where she's been. I did an entire semester on communicable diseases in mortuary school. It's unlikely, but. What if. What if communication occurs. Becky. I haven't thought this through to the next step. I haven't even thought through the actual step. I couldn't even put my hand on her knee, you know? Her *knee*.

He says nothing. I don't remember this kid's name. Or the name he had when he was a kid. I'm glad he doesn't have a name. Why do I feel I should speak to him? I'm as bad as the rest of the people shuffling above the bones I've buried. Me and all the rest of the noisy transfers. Those I've buried do not trouble me with their stories. They do not rise up and sing for me. Oh. Hello Onlybones. I see that you are lonely bones. I roll the kid back. I can't go home yet. She isn't even home. At the library. A library. I don't know where she is. Maybe she's with someone. I feel like she will look into my face and know. Just know.

BECKY

"Is that woman all right?"

"Is she homeless?"

"She doesn't look homeless. Maybe she's drunk. Maybe we should help her."

"Maybe we should leave her alone."

"I feel like if I was mostly passed out in the library stacks I'd want someone to help me."

"I would try not to be in that situation in the first place."

"Miss? Miss, are you okay?"

"Mmph?"

PART 3
LOKI'S BROOD

when you live through something you don't think of it as history
—MARTY GERVAIS

ATHENE'S JOURNAL

The story will. I am the daughter of a man who killed his wife. This will not change. I grow and fester, the story is perhaps more limited.
I have a fascination with the men who touched her body. Who took her. The blood in throats.
Putting language to murder.
It is, perhaps, a failing. we are our failures
as much as we are anything
it is our introduction
when a person, of sound memory and discretion, unlawfully killeth any reasonable creature in being and under the king's peace, with malice aforethought, either express or implied

I believe in predation. In malice. I believe in ambition in all its forms. I can take control of the things before me. I can say and so it will go like this and shape it. Something like aforethought.

dyspnoea is a hunger for air, starved malice no
      no not quite but
shape of word into lung into body into I can brthe underwater
you cant cockjob of risefallstop gaspfloatsink upturned rib it
wont matter i am from the seamarried to sea i can go back
the world is bilt with fingernails down amng her bonesremnantsrevenants of breathed damage into vestigial no
i rot you out rhythm pump etc dys dysp
dyspnoea and no lung into water into into
the shape of the word melancholy is a bubble printed in blackedwater
duckheadopeneyesandthisishow it is just thicker it is just wetter
it is fine you can breathe underwater your suspicion as a child
that if you just did it differently it would work youwereright
you amphibious fucking genius you killed my mother
          sklton of a whl
          thickest here in the spacebetween breathes
because why not

      hungermalicedamage yes into

experiment on land a failure i can go back i have an affinity for the shark
      no malice dysp only onlyhunger onl

it's called a transfer

      he tells me it's important to use the term
to distancehe   takes the bodies
it's his job to take the bodies
      says this and shrugs this is just his day
he just collects what needs collecting sonofabitchshrugs he shrugs

sta
re

wolv
malic

a girl a father a wounded deer a monster
face whittled by rural alberta wind and the smells of his deaths
the things he did or saw he would never say life whittled by
living inside himself
but said take responsibility for death
 he shot it but i was there i was part of it my hands on its flank
still breathing
no struggle but there
if there's blood on your hands then get it on your hands
might as well get blood on your hands if there's blood on your
hands girl
his knife in my hand not cold i thought it would feel cold
didn't look at me there was no moment of poetry where i
looked into animal eyes
it just breathed we breathed it stopped i stopped it
there was an artlessness to it
years later trying to explain artlessness to the man who took my
mother's corpse
trying to define lack, outline failure but my father showed me
death
        introduced us and said take responsibility and i did
i killed that deer he killed my mother these are just facts and
reports filed
i have a hunting license
accept but do not remember do not understand
but responsible
i took it into my hands i came to understand it is best if we do
not understand

sally enswood was not allowed to read wonder woman
comics because her mother said she dressed like a slut
        wonder woman, not sally
although later sally as well but she got over it and i run into her
from time to time at the supermarket
           the bird conservatory where we smile and she
introduces me to some idiot whose name i forget by the time
we break eye contact

my father would buy me wonder woman comics sometimes
 a newsie he had to pass on his way to work and he would
bring them home thumbed through with fingerprints of gore
so i knew he had read them on his lunch but i didn't care
she was beautiful and could throw a car at people
punch a man through a wall
        blam kersmash sounds that made sense to me in childhood
        mrs enswood could say what she wanted sally's father was a drunk and she never once
threw a car at him
        my father killed my mother when i was nine years old.
he choked her to death with his bare hands.
he had been to work that morning had brought me home a
wonder woman comic
it had a backup story with batman in it and i like him too but
he can't throw a car at people

sally asks me how my family is we haven't kept up oh they
are fine
laughs and remembers my wonder woman lunchbox
i never had one but i nod laugh too
it is alright to confuse the details of memory with people you
don't care about
        to ask people if they still like wonder woman
the water
you boil and pour onto ants
thickly singing

i want
to spread
your ribs
like legs
and fuck
your heart
to death

baby with a blooded deer's head
the shapes i see behind my eyes hollow snakes ascending
look force myself to look say no god i did not want this
but did what did i want what did i expect

        dear ants i regret to inform you the world is murder in
animal hands and i

I am lucid and horror is everywhere

not jörmungandr poison darkened sky
or fenrir wolf the blood in savaged throats
        and i hel wait just a girl and so lonelycondemned

wait
only mischief? and yet endbringing
        through murdermorethanmischief

the only photograph I have her armslength part of his face only

he fades she rots and smiles out from frame

i have wanted you to map my body
to prove that i can make you
chart the hulks of shipwreck and reef
to trace lust and malice through seabed
breast and ridge of hip
to draw you within
cage of deadnails
stare into static
at grass
stucco
and you *will* see patterns
the virgin in toast
math among leaves

you understand in sequence
a whale pursued by boats in clouds
this is a failing but an intentional one

if you look into the stubble of his jawline the sharp edges of teeth

of course you think there has to be a reason
      Why did my father kill my mother? Because of patterns in static. Because he stared at grass and leaves. Because he counted numbers and traced arcs through the air.

So, so
the idol dyspnoea hyoid
not quite yet dead
the hun (from blood in throat)
the prince of huaiyang
czarina and strong boy along
lead git in jesus christ pose
mother disney despite letters
tis well

castulus, saint of the sand
took by the throat the circumcised dog
and smote him thus

I will list my father's murders

my mother (the blood in throat)
boiled tribes of ants

spiders (commissioned work I share this guilt)
twenty-eight flies
a rabbit but it should not have run out
a deer coauthored
dream myself into his mind says   i found you there the kitchen
the girl outside
playing among swarm and rats
but here i find you

safe the hollow of your face and throat
wasps pumping venom into rodents
we stitch books into one another's backs
open like wings pages
but there are always birds

author one another other and find the blood in throats

the girl outside and remember
only the smallness of your stiches
the heat and buzz of wing

and I hel wait

rather i were the serpent
        the wolf or wolves to swallow suns
but a daughter left alone

had I a brother I would wolflike savage him
tear free his throat and bind you in his entrails

so I wait among fingernails.

the words bridge between the words span whalebone hate

Language a failing but an intentional one.

wolves, architects, etc. we have been here before

language can't communicate the human brain
so many shitty attempts
hunger for breath through lungs through

communication difficult among monsters

let's just talk about our feelings and our families and our lives and our jobs and everything and just talk forever it will be so great we will definitely solve some things

                    you will not speak of your malice

you will answer no questions
                              Good for you asshole

there is still
what lives within you between jaw and hands what needs
feeding
life   in   browns   and   tans   in   sepia   tone   fade
of whisker men getting older smelling of men getting older
life not as vivid among monsters as perhaps you'd hoped
photographs   you   took   but   in   them
i   own   the   scrotum   swell   of   knuckle   your   wings
one sharp tooth only

745.6 (1) Subject to subsection (2), a person may apply, in writing, to the appropriate Chief Justice in the province in which their conviction took place for a reduction in the number of years of imprisonment without eligibility for parole if the person
(a) has been convicted of murder or high treason;
(b) has been sentenced to imprisonment for life without eligibility for parole until more than fifteen years of their sentence has been served; and
(c) has served at least fifteen years of their sentence.
Exception — multiple murderers

her singing voice nothing special but remembrance serves us so well her life for 15 years. he could be released right around my 25th birthday. younger than she was

when ian took her body

there in the kitchen
the final time I saw them
the heat of wing

on our fridge a calendar dates they will not make
he will go to prison you to the ground
me

but they do not speak i see them through window toys abandoned
garden undefended neck
 i can almost feel the warmth in his hands
his lips only kiss your neck travel
butterfly knife of shoulder
your ribs abandoned playground equipment
the world built within the skeleton

outside
swarm and venom
press against him i trust the words of your skin

IAN

Athene is horrifying. Some days I feel like she has intentional control over me. That she has scripted every gesture, every shift of weight, tilt of hip to keep me looking for her mother. Giving her rides. Doing her favours. Other times she just seems seventeen. Like she's young, those goddamn purple fingernails like she's never seen another damn colour. And her tough talk about malice. Seems like an act to protect herself. To. I don't know. Telling horror stories is one way to avoid telling true stories, maybe. Other times I'm just a dirty old man and there is still some part of me that believes we'll. I don't know what. But something. Some progress. She let slip that she actually saw the murder. I thought she had only found the body. That wasn't in the original report. I remember that from the transfer. Which I can't find.

And Becky threw a bottle at my head the other night. She doesn't know about Athene, she was just drunk. She screamed math at me and wheeled a bottle into the archway behind my head. I'm spending a lot of time at the parlour when I can. Telling my stories to the transfers.

IAN

PART 4
EVERY PLACE I HAUNT IS BORING

Only animals live entirely in the Here and Now. Only nature knows neither memory nor history. But man—let me offer you a definition—is the storytelling animal. Wherever he goes he wants to leave behind not a chaotic wake, not an empty space, but the comforting marker-buoys and trail-signs of stories. He has to go on telling stories. He has to keep on making them up. As long as there's a story, it's all right. Even in his last moments, it's said, in the split second of a fatal fall—or when he's about to drown— he sees, passing rapidly before him, the story of his whole life.
—GRAHAM SWIFT

PART 4
EVERY PLACE I HAUNT IS BORING

IAN

It was me. I eradicated Athene's mother. Part of the reason Jarrington took me on here was because I know computers. Or, I know them well enough to impress the Jarringtons, who are at a basic email and Google level. Only the kid, Jan, uses the billing system or the arrangement planner I set up on the computers. Old Jarrington scratches everything out with a pen and a calculator and Young Jarrington gives his paperwork to me or his daughter to input and file. I computerized their records. Also, because online storage five years ago wasn't what it is now and because the rigs they had in the funeral home at the time were archaic, I purged some material as I was going. Athene's mother was in there.

Apparently I hadn't worked it out right at the beginning, because the first three months or so of transfers I was on are not in the system. Just nothing there. It's possible there are paper records locked in Old Jarrington's filing cabinet behind his desk. But. Well those are locked in Old Jarrington's filing cabinet. How the hell do I ask to go rooting around in there? There's this underage girl I want to bang, sir, and she'd like it if I could go into your records. I erased her mother. I took her and I erased her.

Vince prepped her. If she was cremated he would have burned her, I wouldn't have been doing that yet (why can't I remember for sure?) but I was likely at the service. Thrift store black suit, muted tie, nothing flashy, no jewellery except for the cheap watch set to the wrong time that I hadn't yet broken on a stretcher. Hands clasped before me patient and professional. I am at most of the services if the back of house isn't busy. Help with set up and tear down. Occasionally I'm called on to help lower the casket. Place the receptacle. There as a runner for whichever Jarrington is running the show. Quiet and polite in the background. I shake hands when approached but mostly attempt to fade into background. Just another sombre-faced man in a black suit at a funeral. Resist the urge to check my phone. Suddenly I'll be visible. Someone will complain to Jarrington. Respect and professionalism are pretty much the only things that keep people from treating us like ghouls. Cling to it. Do nothing. Go nowhere. But be there if something is needed; drive Jarrington around, run back to the parlour to get some papers. The old man's glasses. Once (only once) we got to the site without the urn. Old Jarrington stalled with paternal small talk while I tore back to the parlour, nearly red-lining the black sedan on the back county roads. A kid on a bike. I didn't see him in the shade of some trees. I could have killed him. Swerved, raced on. Shaken but nothing happened. Nothing happened but I could have killed him. We would have been the closest funeral home. Probably would have handled the arrangements.

    I was probably there when Athene's mother went into whatever ground Athene's mother went into. But I don't remember. Was busy trying to look professional. To look good during the first days of my go-nowhere career. I can't find her.

    And, in my go-almost-nowhere career, I have had a lot of time to look. I've been avoiding the house. Avoiding Becky. I have been avoiding Athene too, really. She texts constantly. Any news? How R U? Want 2 C bird sanctuary Friday? Becky cocking her eye at the near-constant vibration coming from the end-table on my side of the couch. But with the new position, she believes it's work. I think. Young Jarrington micro-managing me. I keep the vibration turned off now. Every reverberation guilt. The vibrations were driving Laika insane, anyway. She would bark and attack the door, thinking the noise was someone outside the house.

I hadn't wanted a dog. I didn't want to grow accustomed to the specific way it walks and circles when it needs to shit. A grown man encouraging and petting a beast for the act of timely defecation. And then the privilege of handling the leavings. The brown mucousy warmth as I reverse a baggie, enveloping my hand over it. But Becky had wanted a dog. Perhaps subconsciously wanted something to keep us cleaved to one another. I had said a dog, a puppy, means we'll be tied down. If we get a dog we can't go anywhere. And she had looked at me. Asked where I planned on going.

And so Becky bought a dog. On the way home from the library one day she stops at the Pet Planet next to the Safeway and buys a dog. She didn't buy groceries. There's never anything in the house. A bitch we named Laika. And yes, of course I almost instantly adored the little creature and had to feign indifference to avoid smug I-told-you-so's from Becky. A little squash-faced Shih Tzu or something mix that loves us unconditionally even though we are monsters. She never speaks, she just follows me from room to room, looking up and wagging and enjoying me quietly. When Becky is gone to the library or wherever I bury my face in Laika's fur and think about saying ridiculous things to her. How much she means to me. That I love her. I don't actually say them. She is a dog. She would not appreciate any story I would tell her. She does not have that need. She does understand the word "cookie," though. Alright, sometimes I talk to her.

Shortly after getting her, Becky had said, "The first time you make a bitch joke I'm leaving you." Joking. Throwaway line. I wanted to test it. Make the joke and let it hang in the air. I could have said something else. Could have called it what it really was. Said couples get dogs or have babies when they should just break up. Something that needs them when they suspect they don't need each other. I didn't say it, which is just as well. Jarrington's is a family business. Old Jarrington has twice asked me to remind him what my wife's name is. When I told him we're just dating he pretends to be embarrassed by his mistake. Oh that's right. You're not married. Right right. Well, you know. And he leaves it there. Subtle old man that he is. Has commented before that Vince was *never* really right for the parlour. Wasn't a family-oriented man.

Vince was fired. The back of house, the basement, is mine now. Sort of. Vince was not fired because he was not a family-oriented man. Jarrington's revisionist history serves mainly to soothe transition tensions. Vince was fired because we cremated that accident transfer before all the family who had wanted to see the remains had signed off. They were advised that they did not really want to see the mess their loved one had left (although not in those words) but, unexpectedly, a brother came forward saying that he wanted to see it. Of course, by that time there was not much to see. A few bone fragments splintered apart by the heat that didn't ash properly. Cremains. The family had not signed the order yet, we just assumed that they would. Barring the wrong body in the wrong grave or the absolutely fantastic like corpse-fucking or something, this is about as bad a sin as a funeral home can make. The public tolerates us ghouls. They do not love us. We do not want to be in the press. Lawsuits were threatened. A head had to roll to mollify the family.

Vince did not go quietly. He pointed out that it was me who had said that there was no way the family would want to view a completely transected body. He pointed out that Young Jarrington had signed off as manager and given him the authority to cremate. Old Jarrington pointed out that Vince had pressed the button. That he should have known better. My phone had vibrated against my leg during the argument and I had to resist the urge to check Athene's message.

The pile of ashes' family was furious and someone had to go. Jarrington obviously wasn't going to blame his kid, and I, for once, was grateful to be just a trainee. My lack of authority or real importance meant firing me wouldn't appease anyone. I couldn't be blamed. No one questioned me about why I was in such a hurry to be gone that night. To see Athene. I had told Vince to do it although I knew, strictly speaking, that he shouldn't. Of course, he knew that as well as I did. Still. Guilt isn't logic. It is everywhere.

Vince got drunk and came back during a service in the parlour. He interrupted an old woman with dementia who had lost the plot of her speech and was talking about buying eggs. The grandchildren fidgeting. To stop her from speaking would somehow seem wrong. It would break the rules and the quiet rituals of the place. Vince busting in was almost a relief for them. He screamed at all of us. At the staff. At the family. The police were called. Vince will likely never work in the mortuary field again. He's not family and he sank ten years into a parlour that obviously won't be giving him a recommendation. He'll be lucky to work somewhere just doing transfers.

Meanwhile, I have been promoted. Sort of. Old Jarrington took the staff change as an excuse to reorganize the structure and responsibilities in the home. He made up a new title for me: Junior Funeral Director. I'm not a transfer agent or a trainee. I'm not an "embalmer" like Vince was. Jarrington explains it to me like he's doing me a favour. Embalmers don't really exist in the industry anymore, he says. The odd person with good connections and a specialization in corpse preparation might become what they call a "trade embalmer" and basically work freelance for parlours, but this is becoming rare. And is, Jarrington assures me, almost a retirement project for old undertakers who want to keep busy. Old fashioned and outdated and little more than a hobby. A hobby. Vince was an oddity, he says. It was good of him to keep Vince on in that role without any other real responsibilities for as long as he did. Back of house specialists are increasingly uncommon in the industry, he tells me. Everybody has to sell. Everybody has to be able to handle the customers. Our industry is changing, he says. He says our. He says me becoming Junior Funeral Director with a sub-speciality in back-of-house operations is actually better for me in the long run. Career-wise, he says. He doesn't say that he's paying me less than Vince to do Vince's job and most of my old job, too. That with all those responsibilities

I'll still be expected to sell and interact with the front of house. To pick up his idiot son's slack. He doesn't have to say it.

Old Jarrington assures me that we'll hire a couple of transfer guys and get a new trainee in "as soon as the money allows it." But he only advertises for one transfer agent. The legal minimum—he'll send me out to transfer. To train the new person. I'll be transferring, training, prepping, and updating the few certifications Vince had that I still don't. Nothing like a good 15 hour day without breaks to remind one that one shouldn't have been stupid enough to select mortician as a career. It is more money than the trainee position was, though, and I'm busy enough to have believable excuses for avoiding Becky and Athene. So. Progress.

I tried texting Vince about the trade embalmer thing. Maybe he could do that if he still knows anyone from his school days or something. The message bounces back undeliverable so either he's blocked me or he can't afford his phone anymore and has cancelled it. Or, I guess, maybe he's just changed his number but as I'm outlining the possibilities to the remains on the silver drainage table in front of me, I can't bring myself to believe in best case scenarios. The transfer does not seem convinced, either. Sepsis is one of the worst things on the table. Up there with tissue gas, gangrene, and bed sores. Blood spurt. Too much vein tension after we've added another three liters to him. Some remains need a lot of preservative. He doesn't complain. Listens to the story.

BECKY

The pattern and plan. The arc and shape of how a life is supposed to play out. Life on the nose a little too on the nose. Mom thinks he's nice. And just so on and so on and on on andononon. He was lying on the floor of the bedroom when she came in tonight. Just lying there facedown not sleeping just being still and quiet in a place. Said what are you doing, he said nothing. The dog thinking it was a game sniffing at his face and excited. How was your day, he said from the carpet. Monotone, flat, living in his head living in that funeral home basement living anywhere but with her. Which more and more is fine, it's not his fault he's sad, or it is but he doesn't have to deal with himself she does. Mom doesn't dad doesn't. Something will have to happen. She will leave or else marry him because that is what people do when they don't know what else to do. Where to go. What stories to tell. She couldn't face his mother if she were to. Yes, we are so happy. To placate Ian she said I'll order pizza he said thanks and she walked out of the room and she doubts he noticed. There is a tyranny in other people's sadness. How boring a thing to discover.

The crush of lips the crush of a weight on top of me. A man? A woman? Becky needs to sex up her story. Needs to plot the Ravager ravaging. Whiskey smell whiskey eyes now closed now whiskey. She is in her story and veins same as the booze. Edits keep them apart. Other parts edited out to fit the sequence. To put them together. They poison each other and crush. The immodest creaking of jalopy suspension below them, the half moondark of river before them. This is what she wants in this moment. In this moment she is the poison of a thousand lives. A million. She is expansive, no downward arc. Breathe in breathe her crush. These things she knows of Misty. These things she has made up or wants to live.

Laika paces near the door but she doesn't really need to go out, she's just bored, too. Becky should walk her more. Doing nothing breeds doing nothing. Laika's okay in the yard. Ian goes to work all day and the dog's just her problem. He wanted a dog, too. She picks up her shit and brushes out her mats all day while he's at work, but it's him she wants to curl up with when he comes home. He reminds Becky they need supplies in the house. Could she pick up poop bags and dogfood when she does the shopping? Slight emphasis on *when*. Doesn't say she hasn't picked up food *for him,* he uses the dog to make his point. *Laika needs things*. Yes, she does.

IAN

One night I took Athene to the church, the night Athene introduced me to her mother's headstone and asked me to help her find her mother's remains. That night I came home guilty and tried to. Well I didn't try hard. I walked into the house meaning to tell Becky everything. I suppose there isn't actually much to tell but I wanted her to know that I'd been talking to Athene. That I wanted. Something. That something had to change. My job, her (getting a) job, her academics, us, I don't know. She had been slumped down in the chair glass-eyed as George Jetson whizzed to work. Her doctoral proposals scattered around her feet. Laika shut up in her crate so she wouldn't disturb the papers. Becky drunk as shit, dress half-slipped down one shoulder. Paper flowers in her hair looked like an idiot's work. A child's amusement. The bottle had dangled from two fingers. My money the bottle. My money the clothes. Her face slack the glass seeping into her eyes but her mouth small and darting. Her fingers twitch the bottle.

"I'm not like Jane," she said.

Jane?

"Jane Jetson. Space housewife." I consider saying something here. Don't. She continues, "but I'm not really like the Ravager, either." I thought she was waiting for me to respond.

Are you okay?

"No, you're doing it wrong. We're not trying to find the fracture. To establish that there is one. We take that as a given.

It's a starting point, not an end." She had gestured with her hands. Her nails unpainted, but better shaped than Athene's chewed purple nubs. The hand not as delicate, but also not as grubby. With women we're supposed to pay special attention to the hands. I've probably cleaned and painted nails more often than Becky and Athene have combined.

"Like your job. When they call you there is already a body. You don't establish death or that someone will die. You do the next part. You tell the next story. The next value in the sequence that maps the arc." She killed her drink. I was still in the doorway. "Am I supposed to be a storyteller?"

No. You're not. You don't have to—

"And what the fuck would you know about it? What research have you done? Have you done the math?"

And the bottle bounced off the archway next to my head. Laika barking sharply. Once.

"The numbers spiral out. They compound and" she had started to push herself up from the chair. "I really expected that to break." Her eyes on the bottle.

Great.

I walked back out the door and got in my car. Becky calling from the door to come back. She hadn't meant it.

If I had known where Athene lived I would have gone to her. I went to the funeral home. That was the first night I told stories to the transfers. I wheeled one out. Had a look. Had a talk. What had the transfer wanted? Grew up expecting happily ever after but what does the monster expect? Not a lot of people get happily ever after, but they do die. They get the monster death. They wait and grow their fingernails. You are among monsters.

0113581-321

Township of Coaldale Police Department

Lethbridge Regional Police Service

COMPLAINT/ARREST AFFIDAVIT

For joint RCMP action reports use form 3215959-565

Pour français utiliser le formulaire 220223-015

DEFENDANT INFORMATION

Name (Last, First, Middle): DANIELS, Robert Henry	
Alias: NA	Phone:
Current address or Identification on Defendant:	
City: Coaldale	Postal Code:
Sex: M	Weight: 190
Scars, Tattoos, Distinguishing Features:	NA
Hair: Dark Brown, Receding	Ethnicity: Caucasian
Arrest Date: 8/7/2006	Arrest Location: Residence

SCENE INFORMATION

Lead Officer (Rank, Full Name, Badge No.): CPL Russ D'ANGELO 74494274

Additional Officers Present (Ranks, Surnames):	
	Case No: 4922-04
CPL WILLIAMS	
Complaint Reported:	FILE ALL WITNESS INFORMATION USING FORM 3222259-001

Township of Coaldale Police Department

Lethbridge Regional Police Service

COMPLAINT/ARREST AFFIDAVIT

For joint RCMP action reports use form 3215959-565

Pour français utiliser le formulaire 220223-015

Other Services on Scene (Fire, Ambulance, Hazard, Removal, etc.):

Removal—Jarrington

OTHER SERVICE PERSONNEL MUST COMPLETE AND SIGN FORM	Defendant Acquired at Scene: Y
3223568-003	
Charges Filed: Y	Charges:

Distressed call—def. apparently called in. Vic strangled identified as ▓▓▓▓ Minimal struggle. Potential witness on scene—daughter ▓▓▓▓. Def and Potential Witness uncommunicative recommended remand minor ▓▓▓▓ with evaluation to be performed ▓▓▓▓

BOOKING INFORMATION

Booking Officer: Constable First Class R. THORSSON

Date of Booking: 08/07/2006	Prints Taken: Y

ATTACH ALL COMPLAINANT, WITNESS, AND EVIDENCE REPORTS USING FASTENERS ONLY DO NOT STAPLE

IAN

Jarrington frowns across his desk at me. He didn't ask me to sit down when I came into his office and now I've been standing too long to just sit down. Now it's been long enough that he must be aware that I'm standing. Still standing. So he's decided to keep me standing. Deciding each moment to continue. I'm suddenly aware of my fingers and the length of my arms. My hands hang all the way down to my thighs. Almost to my knees. Is that normal? Should my arms just be hanging down? No. But if I cross my arms that means something. I don't know anything about body language, what does that mean? Combative or confident or. I put my hands in my pockets. Does this seems too relaxed? He is my boss but if I take my hands back out then I look fidgety. Also if I take them back out I'll probably wring my hands or crack my knuckles or something else that I'll become horribly conscious of as I do it. Jarrington frowns on. I feel guilty. I must look guilty. I haven't done anything but

"I don't think it's a good use of your time, Ian."

Well. It's just. I mean, records are important. They could be requested and if—

"They could be. But in…what? 37 years? In 37 years I've had a request for records all of twice. And that was only for taxes."

Okay but.

"Look, son." And he leans forward. This must be where he waves me to a chair. Tells me to sit. But no. "Look, you did a good job on those records. God knows things run smoother with you and Janet using the computer to keep track of things for us. You poking through my filing cabinets—again—because you missed something doesn't sound like a good use of your time. Or, and I mean, let's face it here, son, of the time I pay you for."

The old man isn't subtle. Still doesn't wave me to a chair. Keeps talking. I shift and lean slightly against the doorsill.

"That stuff is all in storage and a pain in the ass to get to. We'll worry about it if anyone asks but honestly, who cares?"

Who cares.

"We get paid so people don't ever have to worry about this stuff again, Ian. That's what we do. We sell rest. Peace."

Cheesy old bastard. No wonder the families love him. The man is built of platitudes and handshakes. And meat and blood. A man his size, it would take forever to drain the viscera from his body. If rigor sets in on a man like him you have to fight the body. Position it between workbenches and force the muscles to bend. Break the rigor try not to break the bones. Tight musculature increases vascular pressure. Diverts the embalming fluid from where you want it. The noisy transfer rabbits on.

"If anyone cared they would have asked years ago. I don't care. Not enough to be paying you to go dicking around in the storage shed, anyway."

I could offer to do it on my own time but there is no way that won't raise questions. I feel like I'm already taking risks. Why? Because I want to help a young girl. Is that true? Or do I want to fuck a young girl. What the hell is wr—wait did Young Jarrington file the paperwork? Or not file the paperwork? He was there with me. A burial somewhere I don't remember and gone. Only bones. But he might remember. He probably won't because he's an idiot but I have to remember to ask him. Somehow. Hey, buddy, remember that one woman we buried five years ago? I only ask because I want to bang her daughter, you see, and she'd think it was a favour if I could find her remains. Need to figure out some way to ask this.

I nod. Mumble yeah. Yeah no. No you're right. Some other junk. Tell him I should get back to the prep room.

"Yeah, good idea. We're busy enough without making work for ourselves." I stop leaning. Shift my weight to go. "Oh, kid. Ian. That reminds me." I had half-turned, ready to nod and agree myself out of the old man's office. I turn back. Jarrington pulls a folder out of the stack of papers on his desk. Some fall on the floor. My plan to make the office paperless by 2012 has gone poorly.

"Here, son. I want you to go through this." He hands me the folder. I flip the cover open.

Resumes? Oh. For a new transfer guy?

"Yeah." Jarrington drops papers back into what are more or less piles on his desk. Laughs. "Or transfer girl."

A woman applied?

"Schoolgirl, judging by her resume."

I'll know the last name she goes by from her resume. Her guardians. Maybe her address. It was a protestant church her mom's fake stone was buried at. If I use that maybe I can figure out. What? What are you finding out, Ian? What will you do? Google her? Stalk her? What the hell is— flip and flip through. It's not here.

She's not. I don't see a woman's name here.

The old man laughs again, rearranges the chaos on his desk. "I threw it out."

Because she's a woman?

The old man fixes me with a glare. I should watch my mouth. He's not my friend.

"Because she was a kid, Ian. She was young and had no relevant experience. You want a kid working here?"

Your kids work here.

It's out of my mouth before I think about it. Well. Shit. Okay. Okay, so I'm fired. I'm just fired. Been squirrely lately and questioning and now belligerent. The old man will

But he laughs.

"Yeah, yeah they do. But a mortician's kids grow up with this. My dad showed me his prep room when I was six. An old man on the table. I even knew him, I think. Back then the chemicals were less sophisticated. And less safe. The whole parlour stank of formaldehyde in the winter because we couldn't keep the windows open. Sometimes they put milk in the chemicals because they thought it would hide jaundice. It doesn't, by the way. It just spoils and adds another smell to the place." I've been to mortuary school, old man. Thanks.

I'm still standing. He's telling me about his childhood amongst chemicals and cadavers. While I fantasize about a minor. I don't remember what I said the first time I was asked what I wanted to be when I grew up. I might have said veterinarian. I don't think I said I wanted this. But if I worked in a vet's office I'd just be hauling dead dogs instead of dead people. It all transfers.

Jarrington tells me to look through the resumes, pick one or two to interview. Look for skill sets other than just hauling meat. Someone with a sales background, maybe. I ask him if I should be paying attention to kids with mortuary science training and he shrugs. He's not worried about the kid going anywhere in the industry. At least he's not looking to replace me. I wonder why his kid isn't doing this. The hiring. I wonder why he doesn't just retire. I wonder a lot of things. I think about the shape and shadow created by Athene's padded bra pressing against her shirt. I think about changing Laika's dog food so her shits are less greasy. I think about what I should eat for lunch.

I begin the process of aspirating the bodily fluids from someone's grandmother. My stainless steel drains gurgle her viscera as I tell her about the slight bump on the bridge of Athene's nose. Hazel eyes and cheap makeup poorly applied. I should know, I'll have to do a much better job on my audience's makeup if I don't want to get screamed at by the old man. Athene's figure almost boyish. My audience listens, her own blueveined sacs displaced by the spike I've inserted in her chest. I fire up the centrifugal pump as I describe the freckling of neck and the very top of chest. Veterinarian. I looked into the program after my first year of mortuary science. Didn't really have the grades but wanted to look. More than half of all vet techs quit within a year of beginning their training. Sweeping up shit and putting dogs down is not the cuddly profession the trainees envisioned. Not what I envisioned. I have no idea what I wanted. I heave the desiccated old woman onto her side to facilitate drainage. I'm normally more gentle. I need to calm the fuck down. The grandmother doesn't complain. Doesn't talk about buying eggs or going for a visit. Gracious old thing. What did she want to be when she grew up? Not meat on my tables. No one wants this.

When a church doesn't have its own yard or the family doesn't have or want a plot there, there are a dozen small cemeteries we use regularly. Jarrington owns or has a share in a lot of land. Fields of bones and ashes. It's actually not hard to get land declared a cemetery, especially in the county. There are forms and a few fees, but provided the land is independently owned and there is no reason the land should not be rezoned, like it's uphill of a water source or something, the land is simply designated a burial ground and then it's protected under the cemeteries act.

The church with its little plot probably went up quietly. Few people love the idea of seeing gravestones from their back porch, but there is rarely real resistance. In neighbourhoods where there would be a fight—newer high-class residential zones where the upper-class residents would organize and petition against a cemetery—the land is too expensive to buy up anyway. No, the rich don't get buried in their own backyards. In their own neighbourhoods. And they don't go into the little churchyards in the more modest or older neighbourhoods. The rich are buried out in the country. Great sprawling estates, usually corporate owned (or owned jointly by a dozen small funeral homes and investors). Usually named Restful Meadows or Eversleep Hills. Provides status and transfers the dead away. Out in the country where they can be visited and spoken at on special days. For the other days of the year, the dead are conveniently, reassuringly removed from the living.

Guessing from the house we transferred from, Athene's parents were lower middle-class. I doubt her mother is buried in the big grounds outside of town. No Slumbering Groves for her. Her aunt and uncle might have money if they helped build that church, but that could also be from the proceeds of the sale of the murder house and the land. Athene intimated that she didn't like them. She doesn't live with them. Maybe they turned what she felt should have been her inheritance into a church. Maybe it's something else. In any case, they don't take care of Athene. It's unlikely they paid to put the mother in rich ground. Most likely Athene's mother is in one of our—Jarrington's—own small properties. It's the cheapest option for the mourners that we still profit enough off of to recommend. She is most likely buried a bike ride away from where Athene sleeps. And she doesn't know. I don't know. I can't remember.

The funeral would most likely have been modest. Murders suck for getting paid. Insurance has to go through victim services and victim compensation, which can take a while and usually means the family can't pay much at the funeral. Bodies don't wait around for paperwork to clear. This also means it takes a while for us to get paid, if we ever do at all. People tend to move after violent crimes. We've had invoices returned to sender. Wrong address. Some payments default. Some of the corporate chains take your credit card up front, but Jarrington is old-fashioned. Sends out an invoice and a personalized letter after the fact. Most people pay. It's a small town. Defaulting looks bad. Causes gossip. But not everyone cares, and they are less likely to care after violence. They just leave. And what are we going to do? Dig up the corpse? Dump out the ashes, rinse the urn, and sell it again? One slightly used receptacle on display in the showroom. No, all that really happens is that their name goes in one of Jarrington's books. Gets lost somewhere in the pile of paper on his desk. About once a year when he cleans his office he sends reminders if he has addresses to send to. Grumbles about contacting a collection service about old accounts. I'll believe it when I see it.

BECKY

Becky is sitting on the floor with her papers spread around her. Laika, thinking it's a game, nips at the folders. Wags tail and darts around. Ian pats Becky on the head in what he must think is an affectionate gesture. She ignores him so Ian turns his attention to the papers. Ian picks up a sheet.

"What are you working on?"

"History. Don't mess the piles up, I have to mail this out tomorrow."

"Is this the story about that black smuggler girl?"

Becky rolls her eyes.

"The Ravager."

"And you are…these are graphs? You're graphing her?"

She stops fidgeting with her papers. To her credit, she does not visibly count on her fingers, but there's a small twitch of her hand with each syllable spoken in a broken cadence. Punctuating herself with stops for breath. The twitches pattern spasms into minuscule piano playing.

"I. Am. Plotting. The points of. Where it intersects. Her life, mathematically. Plotting the points of her life mathematically. Assigning values to her milestones so that her progression follows a pattern."

Counts off twitches. 20.

"Damn."

"Isn't that kind of arbitrary?"

She sighs. She could have said "mile" like "my-all" the way Ian pronounces it. But he also says "deck-all" for "decal" and "dialate" when he means "dilate" and she just won't live that way. Abandons the count to failure. Answers him honestly.

"Plotting a life like a story is always arbitrary. Narrative and progression are largely arbitrary concepts, I guess."

"So why do it?"

"It's what's expected. We want a story. A rise and a fall. Arc."

"Okay. But these are spirals."

"The arc doesn't end, Ian. We just chop pieces of it off and call them story. A spiral is just a more persistent arc. History doesn't end."

Ian must wonder here if it would be best to walk away. Leave her to her work. He must smell the booze. There are pictures of nautilus shells among the Ravager fabrications. His curiosity gets the better of him and he presses.

"Are these shells the same thing? Is this pattern the same?"

"What?"

"These, the nautilus shells. Is this the pattern you're using for your spirals?"

"There is a certain margin of error."

Ian puts the graphs and pictures back into the pile on the floor. He leaves Becky amongst her spirals and goes into the bedroom. Falls asleep watching YouTube videos in bed, Laika curled into the bend of his knees. Becky does not come to bed that night. The home menu on *The Jetsons* cycles into the night as Becky chases failed math with rum. She thinks, when Ian patted my head it was the first time he's touched me in months, which is not exactly true. But it is close. The golden spiral has largely been disproven as any kind of significant presence outside of math. It is a pattern that exists in nature except when it doesn't. Like all patterns. It exists in some places but doesn't exist in most. Like any pattern. Nautilus shells do *not* spiral outward in curves that have a golden ratio between their chambers. The math does not support it. But people think they do, and people retell the false statistic. Which is the same as being true. Patterns exist if we say they exist. Faces in stains and burnt toast. Our brains, architects of nonsense. Because pattern evolved in us. Recognizing the shake in the grass might be a wolf and running has no consequences. If it's a wolf: survival. If it's not a wolf: survival. And so we evolved a need for patterns. See them everywhere because why not. No consequences. Knock back a drink, two drinks, three drinks. Sequential; math has uses. Becky creates patterns. She spirals the Ravager out into the world.

IAN

Are you bodies? Are you even transfers? That nothing word that means. No. Just meat. Heavy quiet meat.

The bones of all I've buried rise up and sing for me. Oh. Hello Onlybones. I see that you are lonely bones.

ATHENE

I think of my father. Stuck there. Doing nothing. Day in, out. Grey walls and costume of sameness. Does he live in that present? Sisyphean or maybe just boring. Or does he live in the past? Relive that day? Does he think of me. Of her.

Does he look ahead? After 15 years murderers are eligible for parole. I will be 27. Younger than she was when. An entire life. And free. Does he live in that future?

He could start a new family. Murder a new wife. Athene is not the name he knows me by. A species of owl I have fashioned myself after. The Bird of Prey Centre has informed me. But appropriate. Born of his mind, his act, if not his head. My last name is that of my first foster parents. Not his. If he ever wrote to me, I was never given the letters. Will he look for me? I will be far from Coaldale. I eagerly look forward to never seeing him. But could he track me? Do they give information to people? To murderers?

I don't understand present or future in him. The future is always difficult. Even the future has fallen into disrepair. But I will claw some value from it. No, in my father I understand the past. Present perhaps in Ian. Sisyphean. He is his own boulder. The dead bodies he moves are not what weigh him down. But my father I understand as a creature of memory. A predator through a window. Lua Saturni or just a hungry animal. I'm not sure what he was gaining strength from. But I will not ask him. I have no wish to be anything to him. Not even vengeance. To have him mean anything to me except a hazy memory. Part of a face in a photograph. I will say goodbye to my mother and I will leave this place. If he comes looking for me he will find only a ship of dead men's fingernails.

BECKY

Becky thinks it is possible that Ian is having an affair, but she is not certain. She is also not certain she cares. Also, is *affair* even correct? she wonders. They aren't married. The social semantics seem more interesting than the possibility. He is spending a lot of time away. He has been promoted, sort of, and it is perhaps responsibility keeping him out. In his basement. Facedown on the bedroom floor. For Becky, it means she can do as she likes. Any night he texts he'll be home late is an excuse not to have dinner ready for him. *K get a burger or somthin on the way if u'll be late* is an entirely reasonable communication somehow. The burden of his own life has shifted back to him. He never explicitly said he expected dinner but it seemed an unspoken agreement. A contract she felt she had to honour. When she speaks to his mother on the phone she says little things. Well, the silver lining of not having a job is it's easier for you two to keep house. And she'd laugh. A little joke. Feed and clean my son. She can't remember the last time she had sex. At first she thought his work had done something to him. But she hears the occasional sound from the other room when he's on his computer. She sees the smash of wadded tissue shoved to the bottom of the garbage. Then she suspected he was having an affair. Frequent texts, frequent absences, infrequent sex. Then she thought he wasn't having an affair, he is simply a sad man who no longer knows how to talk to her. Which she is fine with. The talk is tiring and follows the same curves every time. Except for the rare occasion when the rum makes it seem worthwhile, she doesn't consider initiating. Sex without mystery seems empty. Ian, if he has mysteries, isn't worth puzzling out, she thinks. She loves him, but she does not need him. She no longer wants to need him. They are companionable, like her textbooks told her elderly people are. An accelerated history. The story edited to skip to the next plot point. His being gone leaves her to her real work. Her reading and histories. If the Ravager history works—if she gets into PhD at Bow River—she'll have to move to town. Live in residence and only see Ian on the weekends. Reading week an exciting break. He can drive up with Laika sniffing the foothills from the passenger window. They would have a story, then. Not just the unrelenting plod.

Becky kicks her slipper off for Laika to chase. The dog scrambles, her pads unable to find purchase on the laminate. Tongue-lolling manic chase and retrieval. Dropped slipper and wagging. Becky kicks the slipper away again. Laika scrambles. The pattern and plan. Becky's application, in triplicate, has been sent off. Transcripts have been sent, stamps across the seal declaring their institutional integrity. Ten dollars each. A goddamn scam, Becky had thought. Had wanted to write an angry letter to the Alumni Association, but had gotten over it. She is making plans for leaving. Slow ones, but plans. Ian is a man-child and rarely does any of the banking himself. He won't know how to pay the bills if she leaves. If Becky wanted to, she could take what little money Ian has and vanish. He wouldn't know she was gone for hours. He wouldn't know the money was gone until his debit card failed at some sandwich shop on his lunch break. But Becky does not want to do this. Her story is not a random stab out, not a running away. It is the building of momentum, of arc. This is simply a fallow period. A part that should be edited out. Becky has faith in the narrative, if not the pacing. She hopes her letter writers from her Master's degree remember her well enough. They were gracious over email. Promised to send their recommendations. Again.

Confirmed that they had submitted their letters when Becky politely, but feverishly, reminded them that the due date was upon them. The application is in. She has received confirmation from the University of Bow River that her application has been received and thank you very much for your interest. Each application is given careful consideration by a committee of...

And so on. Time has passed. The application is in. Ian is out. Becky keeps working. She has registered with numerous ancestry databanks and has been working diligently to explain her connection to the Ravager. Has created entries for the Berkler brothers and fleshed them out with the material of her studies. Edits to her family tree to show the remove. The connection. Misty she left unaddressed. She thinks it would be better to draw her connection to the brothers. Less obvious than claiming to descend directly from the pseudohistorical figure. When she is at the school, when she is working on her dissertation, Becky will make her mark. She will publish on the Windsor/Detroit smuggling connection and she will present work on figures so important that history forgot them. But not yet. She won't give the story away yet.

Admissions will be contacting her one way or the other any day now. She fears the thin envelope more than her actual family history. The likelihood of heart disease and cancer. A future that seems unreal because of its hopeful remoteness. *The Jetsons* don't get cancer. Much more immediate is the future of envelopes in the mailbox. Another uncle has gotten sick. Will she be coming home to Ontario to visit? She delays answering. Wants to know what her future holds. The mail comes around noon every day, which means that as Becky's clock inches towards two she becomes restless. Pet Laika and try to be still. Watch Netflix and try to be still. Consider walking Laika but instead just let her crap in the yard. What if the mail comes while they're away? There is no arc to stillness and she will frenzy-surge to the door as soon as she hears the mail carrier's heavy boots outside. Becky kicks her slipper again, Laika flying off her lap after it. The phone rings. Becky speaks to a professor at the University of Bow River. She is too flustered to catch her name. Something Asian-sounding, although the voice sounds white. Becky chides herself mentally. That's racist. Wait, is that racist? The professor tells her there is interest in her project but some concerns about it. They haven't been able to track down some of the documents she. Provisional acceptance. There are some questions. Would need to contact the archivist. Veracity. Would Becky mind having a conference call with. The archivist. Very interesting project. Collins previously not. The archivist who lost the photo. Very excited to talk with you about the project. Yes. You too. Becky hangs up the phone and says fuckmotherfuck into the air. Laika waits for the slipper to move again. Lists of things that happen. Assign them a value and a story. Count them off.

IAN

The phone in viewing room two goes. It really can only be Janet in the front office or Old Jarrington wanting something but I'm supposed to answer with patter anyway. So

Jarrington Family Funeral Home. Ian speaking how may I

"Hey Crypt Keeper. There's someone here asking for you."

I look over at the casket on the wheelie. I haven't put the stuffed animal the family brought in with the old woman. Haven't arranged the flower spray. I haven't even put the drape over the glorified gurney we use to wheel the caskets from the prep room to the show rooms. The rusted wheelie has seen better days. Jarrington says we'll get a new one soon. He's famous for his soons. Fuck there is still a ton to do. I look at the wall clock. 9:38. I do math for a moment before I remember that this clock actually means 9:38.

Jan, can you stall them? The McMahons' viewing wasn't supposed to be until 10:30. It's. She's not ready.

"I, uh. I don't think it's the McMahons. It's a girl."

Shit.

Shit. Is she there with you?

"No, she went into the displays. She's looking at the urns."

Mind blanks. Need something. Say something.

"Is she the girl who was going to do the school project?"

What?

Yes. Probably. The school project.

I have no idea what she's talking about, actually. But maybe this won't get me fired.

I'll uh. I'll be right in.

I push the casket on the wheelie out and then roll it back towards me to straighten the wheels. The drape will fall nicely over it now and I can lock the wheels. Family walking nearby on the carpet can sometimes shift the coffin slightly otherwise. If the wheels aren't squared off. Pretty fucking unnerving when the casket lurches or the flowers fall off mid-viewing. The wheels don't quite go. I want to push and straighten again but I need to get to the front room. I lock the wheels. Should hold for a minute until I get back. Just need to get Athene out of the front before Old Jarrington sees her. Shouldn't actually be too hard, really. Old funeral homes are labyrinths. There are sliding walls and side doors everywhere. It's a practical design—if I'm wearing a gory smock fresh from the prep room and I hear a family about to come out of a viewing early, it's good to be able to disappear quickly. If I need to bring an urn out front I don't want to go through the main hallway to do it. Families don't want to see you handling other business. Other remains. When mom is in our care, we're supposed to make it look like she is our only care. Plus, sidestepping crying people is useful. I can get Athene somewhere, find out what the fuck she wants, and get her out before Jarrington sees her. Jan thinks she's here for school, she won't even remember. She'll be playing *Candy Crush* on her phone because that's all she does. Becky complains that her scores are inhuman. I've never played. This is okay.

In the display room, Old Jarrington is talking quietly with Athene. Their heads bowed towards one another near a display of faux-marble urn casements. The big old man dwarfing her, but speaking softly and with minimal hand gestures. She is wearing dress slacks and a blue blouse. High neck. No cleavage. No jewellery. Nails a predictable purple but not chipped. No lipstick. She has a school bag over one shoulder. Jesus Christ. Jarrington sees me. Raises his head.

Sir, I—

"There you are. Ian, this is Athena."

"Athene."

"Oh, I'm sorry. Athene, this is the funeral director I told you about. I told Mrs. Vickers he would show you around."

"Hello, Ian."

Uh. Hi.

I look from face to face. Jarrington has his ready-made smile on. Never know when it's genuine; he's good at this. Athene half-smile. Amused at this at me. What in the?

"Ian just recently took over as a funeral director here and he has a viewing today, isn't that right, Ian?"

Yes. I. Yes. The McMahons are coming in for 10:30.

Jarrington looks at his watch. Chuckles.

"Well, usually that actually means 10:15, so I won't keep you two. Ian, show her how you finish the viewing set-up, will you? That should be good enough for your report, won't it?"

Athene smiles up at him.

"That should work. Thank you so much."

Jarrington gestures her towards the hallway. She precedes us and Jarrington puts a hand on my arm.

"Show her the viewing room and give her a walk through the showroom here while the family is viewing then get her out."

Sir, I—

"It's a favour to her teacher. I'm sorry, it's a pain in the ass, I know, but just help me out here. You're doing *me* a favour."

Yeah. Yeah sure. No problem.

Why the fuck am I getting away with—

"It goes without saying, but I'm going to say it anyway because. Well. She does not go downstairs."

No, of course not.

"She's young and she's pretty and she'll bat her eyelashes and ask. These kids all think they're investigative reporters or something. She'll ask and she'll flirt. Now I know you're not like that but."

No. No, I. She won't. We won't go anywhere.

Athene pretends to examine plaques on the hallway wall. Photos of the little league team Jarrington used to sponsor in the name of community goodwill. Looks back at us and smiles her teeth into my eyes. Jarrington pats me on the shoulder and disappears back towards his office. Jan in the front office is absorbed by her cellphone. Athene in front of me.

This way. Uh no wait, through here.

We duck into a side passage just in case Young Jarrington comes out. One less person to see us, I suppose. Although as we move through the narrow side corridor I'm aware of her drugstore perfume and the closeness of the passage. I turn sideways to squeeze by some piping in the wall. Hand to my chest, holding my tie. As I turn I look at her. I look at the hair tucked behind one ear. Focus on it. Individual strands. I meet her eyes and I want to

The door opens behind her. Old Jarrington squeezing into the small space.

"Oh kid, kid. Ian. Almost forgot. We are meeting with the family before the service this afternoon. You're taking lead with the. Oh shit I forget. Russian name."

Bellanov. Yeah, I remember.

I more than remember, I'm dreading it. Today I do my first service as lead funeral director. It's going to be a big funeral. They are coming in right after the McMahon viewing to consult with me for last minute arrangements. Why are they calling the old man?

You spoke with them?

"Yes, I had the daughter-in-law on the phone today. Told her you would be handling it from here."

Shit. In-law taking control is always a bad sign. I've done enough in the front office to know that. They feel like they have something to prove. Russians?

It's not orthodox, right? It's just that priest. Blokov, right?

"It's just Blok."

We're yelling down this service hallway at one another. Athene trying to flatten herself against one wall to not be between us.

"Don't do that, honey. The walls in here aren't as clean as they should be. Why did you bring her—"

Wanted to show her how we get around. Your son has a view in room one, didn't know if they were coming out.

Jarrington eyes Athene. Dressed at least as nice as I am in my shitty suit, but a seventeen-year-old with a schoolbag and without other family looks out of place. Even accompanying a director.

"Right. Sorry, what did you ask?"

Is it an orthodox service?

"No, Blok doesn't do Orthodox and she didn't say anything about changing anything in the service. Just our chapel and then a viewing, and then a private plot. Just letting me know there is more family coming. And the family is thinking of doing something special."

Athene looks from Jarrington to me. Back. Fiddles with her backpack.

Special? Last minute changes?

"I know. But it's their show. We'll see what they have to say in the meeting."

I thought we were already expecting a large—

"We'll collapse the rooms right after the McMahons leave. After we talk about preparing for the service."

Which means sliding all of the panels apart and turning both viewing rooms into one big room. Which doesn't look great and takes every drape and swath of fabric in the entire house to cover up all the accordion folding screens and other eyesores in the old place that become apparent when they are in the center of one big room instead of the corners of two smaller ones. This is going to take forever. It's not even 10 a.m. and I feel like I'm behind.

The chapel, though?

"It'll work. You'll make it work."

Jesus Christ.

Jesus Christ. Okay. Thanks.

"Right after you finish this I want to talk with you. Get ready for this."

He looks at Athene.

"Right after you show Athena out, I mean. Take your time.

Answer questions. Don't be nervous. Ian's a good guy." She smiles, turns to Jarrington.

"Would I be able to sit in on that service? Or the meeting before? For my report?"

"No, darlin'. The families can be kind of raw at these things." He says it politely, but very firm. Nods and squeezes himself back out of the hallway. Yells something else back to me that I'm sure is a reminder to be quick but I don't hear it. Athene looks at me.

We. Uh. I guess we're fighting the clock. This way. The families can get weird at big funerals. Don't worry, Mrs. McMahon won't mind you being here.

I force a chuckle. She doesn't. We emerge in viewing room two. The coffin is open and Athene starts slightly as she sees what we've done with what's left of Mrs. McMahon.

Oh. Right. There are dead people around here. You should be ready for that.

"Right."

I draw the side panel closed. The door to the main hall is already shut. I'm looking fully at her. She is looking at the casket. I decide. Well fuck it. I go in.

What are you doing here?

"What?"

Eyes go wide in head. Mouth, small predator teeth sheathed momentarily.

This is fucked up, Athene. This is where I work. What is this for? To look for your mom? To mess with me?

She contracts; eyebrows lower. I'm better at applying eye shadow than she is. Of course, the eyelids I'm applying it to do not move. The eye beneath has no flicker or heat.

"What I'm doing here. I'm. I'm doing a school paper, Ian."

She shrugs her bag off her shoulder. Fishes out a notebook and offers it to me. I don't look at it.

Right. A school paper. Shouldn't you be in school right now?

"Look. Asshole. I called your boss for this. Not you. I didn't even know he was going to ask you to show me around. It's legit. I have permission to be here to do research. I'm actually doing—"

You just happen to be doing a school paper on a funeral home and you come to where I work.

"My mother was killed when I was young and I kind of know a guy who works on bodies. It's pretty fucking reasonable that I would have an interest."

It. Well.

"This is extremely not about you."

It makes sense. But somehow the whole thing feels like a trap. Hazels at me. Jesus.

Okay. I'm sorry.

"You complete ass."

I said I'm sorry.

"If I wanted to fuck with you I'd call the girlfriend you're weirdly hiding me from, Ian."

Okay Jesus Christ keep it down.

Can't help but notice she phrased that as "if" she wanted to "fuck with" me. Can't help but notice she thinks it's weird that I hide her from Becky. Like there's nothing to hide. Like she thinks there's nothing to hide. Which, I guess, means there is nothing. I busy myself with Mrs. McMahon. Take the teddy bear from the bag of effects the family provided. Lean the bear against the folded hands. Turn my attention to the stand for the flower spray. Should I use the stand or put a spray up on the foot of the coffin. The family usually doesn't make these decisions, they leave it to us. I'll look at what the florists brought for this one. Young Jarrington did the initial arrangements for the McMahons and I know he's been using Ed and Nellie's Flowers lately. I fucking hate Ed and Nellie. Their arrangements look like shit. And Young Jarrington will have just dumped the flowers on the long worktable in the garage. If he didn't just leave them in a car. What time is it? Jesus I'd better get to those before the cold wilts them. Provided Nellie didn't give us already wilted cast-offs. I've told him to go to Hamil. Hamil knows how much money a funeral home means to a florist. He makes a damn effort. Ed and Nellie just assume we'll take anything because we have to.

"It fell."

What?

"The bear. It fell over."

Oh, thanks.

I fix it. I'll use the stand for the flowers. If they look shitty at least that way they aren't sitting directly on top of everyone's focus. We have a drape that would work better for this coffin.

"You don't even look at it. At her. You look at the stuff around it."

We're under the gun here a bit, Athene.

"And are you not looking at me now?"

I do.

I don't. I don't want to really have a fight or a thing here, okay? I'm working. That was shitty of me, I'm sorry. But like. You have to realize this is weird.

"Yeah, okay. I'm sorry too. I thought your boss would have told you someone was coming in."

You probably should have told me.

"Well. Okay. But I didn't want you to say no or ask me not to."

I jump up and down twice in front of the stand. It's old, too. And the floors. Heavy people trudging by it, maybe brushing against it as they pay their respects. It barely wobbles. Good. I have to get those flowers before they turn from shit to absolute shit. Athene scribbles down everything I do. As I unfold a drape I look up at her.

What about the resume, though.

"What?"

I mean. I can buy that you are doing this because you're curious and, I mean, probably you can get an easy A off of just the sympathy involved here, but applying to work here? That is deeply fucked up.

"I didn't apply to work here."

You didn't.

"No. Jesus Christ I don't want to do thi—" and she stops. "Sorry, I mean I know it's your job, but. Well. It wasn't me."

Jarrington said a teenage girl applied to haul. To transfer.

"There are a lot of teenage girls, Ian."

That want to work at funeral homes?

"There was one at the desk upstairs when I walked in. I think we had sociology together once."

Yeah, well, her last name is on the door.

I think about parroting back to her all of the things Jarrington said about a mortician's kids being different. I don't. I buff the corner of the casket with my jacket sleeve. Did Young Jarrington bump a fucking wall? I know I didn't hit anything. Not with this one.

"Okay. Well. It still wasn't me who applied."

Okay.

"Wait, why isn't that girl at the desk in school?"

Like I said, her name is on the door. She spends her spare periods here. And probably some that aren't spare. That's how small parlours work. They all pretty much live here. We all do.

I think about apologizing again. I don't. She watches me fuss with the drape and arrange the side table. Writes in her book when I fill a pitcher with water. Studies and charts me creating a perfect stillness. A moment freezing and plotting me into it. Getting Mrs. McMahon and me arranged in tableau. Pen scratches away at me. I start rehearsing sales patter in my head. Remember to frame it as what the deceased would want, not what the bereaved want. Athene writing.

BECKY

Ian isn't answering his phone. He had said today was something special. Setting up a viewing. No but wait. He's done that before. He sets up behind the scenes all the time. Today was. What? Becky searches but can not remember. Becky is annoyed to discover that she needs a man. More accurately, she needs a man's voice on the phone. The actual man is fairly unimportant. Which, Becky supposes, makes Ian ideal. He will also most likely lie for her, Becky thinks.

Because the whole thing was a lie, of course. Becky's proposal. The Ravager. Oh, some of it was real. Stories always need trail markers. Babe Trumbell was shot. The fighting Parson got away with it. But no one could prove Misty was there. A name she found in a ledger. A witness who had disappeared. No one could prove she wasn't whom Becky said. As long as she could cover. As long as she could get Ian's voice on the phone. Why the hell had she made up a male archivist? Just as well. While Becky is content to lie to the admissions board, the thought of trying to do a fake voice into the phone is somehow too much. Unseemly. There are lies and then there are lies. There was a Misty. If Ian says he worked at an archive and destroyed a photo accidentally, it could work. They won't check too hard. They don't have time. They've already provisionally accepted me, Becky thinks. But the phone number. She'll have to buy a disposable cell phone. They sell those at any mall, don't they? But no wait, the area code will still be Albertan. But can't you spoof numbers on the internet? That has to be a thing. Or just use the internet. Ian could call through Skype—register his parents' phone number in Ontario and then just call over the internet. Would that work? Becky begins making notes. Writing dialogue for Ian. He has to be familiar. But not too familiar. The project is Becky's project, after all. He is just a worker who knew the materials. Not necessarily the history. Yes. Our histories aren't wrong, we just don't know them. She hates that she would have to admit to Ian her shaping of the history. It wasn't lying, the more she thinks about it. She was simply shaping the history into a story that they weren't familiar with. The problem is that they wouldn't care unless she could make it look like someone else already knew this arc. Becky runs to the front window to check if Ian has taken his car to work. She can't remember if he drove one of Jarrington's home the night before. The driveway is empty. She swears. Tries his cell phone again but no answer. She paces. Composes dialogue out loud. Shapes the arc. Laika wakes from her bi-hourly couch nap and begins following Becky as she patrols. This is a game to be played at this moment for her, Becky thinks.

    She said she'd get the number. That she had it all written down somewhere. Buy a cell phone. Email her the number. Have to look up the email on the university site. She said her name was something Lee or maybe Li. Have to send it today. It looks bad to keep them waiting for information. They won't suspect it's made up. Or they might. They may just think she's unorganized. Would they pass on her for that? Revoke the provisional. Becky's mind spirals as she plots. Laika tries to nip the bouncing laces on Becky's moccasins. She could get a bus down to the mall. Go to the cell kiosk. From there walk to Jarrington's. Everything is close once you get into the town. Ask to see Ian, they'll like that, they're big on the family. No, wait. Taxi would be faster. But just waiting for a taxi in Coaldale can take forever. There isn't exactly a fleet of them. Ask to borrow the neighbour's car. Say it's an emergency. What is her name? Paulene? Paulette? Waiting on her porch while the crows screech their own versions at the magpies. Becky looks at the clock and figures out the time. She could be at the funeral home by the end of the business day. Laika would be fine in her crate by herself, probably. Ian could call in, maybe catch someone in the History office. Or leave a message. That would be acceptable, wouldn't it? If it was left on time. She would have to leave now. Becky tells Laika "bedtime" and Laika scampers into her crate. This too is a game. Becky dutifully moves one of the Goosey Treats from the box on top of the crate down to Laika's eagerness. Shuts the crate and latches it. The dog finishes the biscuit flavoured with goose but for some reason made to look like a femur before turning once on her cushion and immediately snoring. Becky tries Ian's phone again and then leaves the house.

IAN

"What do you think your girlfriend is doing right now?"

Stop it.

"No, really. I like thinking about her. She's a mystery to me. Another part of your weird hidden away life."

I'm trying to work, Athene.

"It's fun. I like making up stories about her. And you."

You're making this weirder than it has to be.

"For you."

Well. Yes. You are making this hard for me.

"Life feeds on life. It makes me stronger."

Swell.

"So what is she doing? What do you think she's doing while you hang out with a girl a dozen years younger than her? Is she thinking about you? Waiting for you to come home? Has she texted you?"

I said stop.

"What is she doing?"

I don't know, okay. Probably watching *The Jetsons*.

"*The Jetsons?*"

Yeah. She loves that stuff. The camp of it. The future.

"The future. Ha. 'I've seen the future, brother. It is murder.'"

You know, for a minute there I thought I was the asshole here.

"What?"

Like me giving you a hard time for being here. That was shitty of me. But it made me forget what you are.

"What I am?"

You're a monster.

"Sure. But I mean. That's boring."

Super. I'm super interested in you finding me boring.

"Jesus, Ian. What is wrong with you? Why are you so purposefully sad? Pick a fight. Get mad at me, don't just fuck with those flowers."

I'm not. I'm not mad. I'm not sad. I'm not anything. It's fine. We just need to get this done.

"You're not anything? Hunh. Are you going to say something about being dead inside? Or like relate that to the funeral home?"

No.

"Okay. Because that would be *entirely* boring. Up till now you've only been mostly boring."

Great.

"I'm in high school. I hear that shit everyday. A lot of existential crisis among 17 year olds. Generally in the girls' change room after gym."

Yeah, you're not sentimental. I get it. But stop trying to prove you're better at this than I am.

"At what?"

At being disconnected. By not having a fuck to give. I get it. You're a tough kid. Shut up about it, maybe.

"There he is."

She scratches her pen at her book. Flips a page and looks back up.

"Okay, tell me about this consult with the family tonight. Before the funeral."

I glare at her. Then decide, fuck it. It's not her fault what I've constructed in my mind isn't what the world actually looks like.

They'll tell us some last minute impossible thing they want. All the grandchildren holding candles or something. Music cues that happen at certain points in the service.

"Why is that impossible? That sounds fairly reasonable."

You know how brides get really controlling about their

weddings? Like they want these specific things to happen at specific times?

"Well. Not just brides. But fine."

Okay, well they make that happen through weeks of planning. Or months. And they rehearse. Funerals get thrown together in a couple of days. Half the people involved are drunk, and no one practices anything.

"People are drunk at weddings."

At receptions, sure. Usually not from the moment they walk in the door. And usually they aren't angry. A lot of people are angry at funerals. At the family, at the deceased, at me because I'm making money off of grief.

"That's normal, though, isn't it?"

Sure. It's normal. It's understandable. It still isn't conducive to making things happen. People don't take directions at funerals. I tell a guy to hold this specific bouquet of flowers and walk at a specific point in the procession, you know what happens? Best case scenario he glares at me. More likely he launches into a mini tirade about me being a bloodsucking fiend. Once a guy took a swing at Young Jarrington.

"Really?"

People get very protective and selfish with their grief. They are suffering and I'm just there for the money. How could I understand. How dare I. Etc. It happens. Ninety-nine percent of the time people are fine, but you start telling them what to do and that math changes. People do not want to be instructed in their grief.

"When my mother died they kept telling me what to do. How to think of it. One even told me how I should remember her. Don't think of her like this, sweetheart. Think of her like. It went on and on."

And I'll bet you fucking loved it.

"—"

Shit, I'm sorry. That was a stupid thing to say.

"It's okay. You're right. I hated it."

Well. But there was a better way to say it, I'm sorry. Anyway. It's fine as long as I'm sycophantic and quietly standing in the back of the hall. Help old ladies get seated. Direct people to the washrooms. Make sure the flowers don't fall over. But when it's more involved than that, when the family thinks they want other people somehow involved, when they think they want ritual and pageantry, it just leads to people getting pissed off. People don't know what they want. And death is confusing. I understand it; it just also makes my workday harder.

"People don't know what they want."

Not in my experience. We gently guide them towards the choices they have to make. But when they think they have a plan, it's usually rash.

"What do you want, Ian?"

Is this? Are you being philosophical, or?

"No, I mean. I guess that way, too. But do you try for what you want? Do you have a plan? Or do you wait around for something to gently guide you."

You're being weird.

"I'm just curious."

Or you're messing with me.

"Well."

Look. Obviously I've. Been interested. Wanted to.

"Obviously?"

Stop it. Look, we've pretty specifically worked around discussing my. This. Whatever. Let's not get into it three feet from remains.

"I just want to hear you say it. I want to hear honesty."

Yeah. Well, we're all waiting for something. Or waiting to not be waiting for something. Can you get that door? I'm gonna have to carry a couple of big sprays of flowers in here and they're going to be delicate as shit.

"Fine."

Great.

Jarrington asks me to sit this time.

"We'll be there tonight, of course, but we're just shaking hands. This is you tonight."

Right. I know.

"Okay but knowing it and doing it are two different things. Everything that happens is on you. A flower is out of place, you need to fix that immediately. Or get someone to do it while you make facetime with the ones paying the bills. You're good to everyone, obviously, but you pay particular attention to the ones running the show. Because the next time someone dies, everyone will be looking to them to take care of things again. And if they trust you, they'll use you again. They'll come here. That's why we don't push the upsells hard here, we want the family, not the funeral. Selling them into a ridiculously overpriced casket and getting all the bells on a service makes a bundle, but it's one time, and it probably leaves them with a bad taste. We want to bury the entire family."

I've heard this patter before. It's the mission statement, if not what is actually always put into practice. Young Jarrington upsells like crazy. Most families are so charmed by his old man they come back anyway. He bought a new Lexus last year. I wonder when the old man will die.

"Alright, so you're decent with people when you have to be, I've seen that. Oh, on that note: thanks for dealing with that girl today. Pain in the ass, I know, but we build goodwill where we can and I know the teacher. She's one of our families. I did services for her husband and both her folks, I think. Maybe the brother. I'd have to look."

Sure. Right, no problem. My pleasure, I mean.

"The next thing about tonight is Blok. He's a dick. As soon as you see him go over and shake his hand. If he's talking to someone else you wait patiently. He'll make a goddamn stink if you don't. He's the holy man and it's a holy event. Don't talk business with him. He'll do services in our chapel but he hates everything about private practice burials. Except cashing our honorarium. He's okay with that. Shake hands, thank him, and remove yourself. I'll deal with paying him and everything else, but you need to start building a rapport so I want you gladhanding him tonight."

Okay. Sure, I can be nice to a cranky priest.

"Don't take it personal if he's short with you. He's like that."

Okay. I won't mess with him.

I laugh.

Vince used to say "don't fuck with holy men. They'll cast cleric spells on you."

"What the hell are you talking about?"

It's just something Vince said. Dungeons and Drag—uh. It's just Vince's nerd jokes.

"Vince doesn't work here. Vince got fired for saying shit like that," says Jarrington, which is not even remotely true. The way he's rewritten history to make it look like he didn't throw Vince under a bus would be interesting if the old man wasn't red-cheek purse-mouth death-glaring at me.

"It's a funeral. We have a bereaved family arriving in a few minutes. Serious up."

Yeah, no. I was just. Right.

"Okay. So what else? Oh right. Flower thing. The family wants to do a flower procession that is clearly going to fail. The daughter-in-law and a few of the immediate family are going to go over it when they come in before the service. It's going to be ill-thought-out and we'll try to steer them away from it if possible, but people get their minds made up. Our main job will be mitigating how bad it is."

The truth is that I'm the person no one here wants to talk to. Old Jarrington gets away with a lot because he's old. People see him as a patriarch. As a businessman. People shake his hand and catch up with him, like he's any other community feature. Death isn't really part of it. They think he doesn't touch the bodies. That he doesn't see and smell everything. People don't understand how a small shop like ours works. He's up to his elbows in everything I am. Everything his son is. Every day. The fluids, the burnings, the dirtiest of the dirty work gets kicked down to us when possible, but if I'm setting up a room or hauling a body and his son is selling or busy with a viewing, Jarrington isn't shy about rolling up his sleeves. You can't be in this business. Too much work to do on a very real timeline. Decomposition happens at a shocking rate. The body is just waiting to go to shit. But he has the patter down. He has the smile. He has what seems like genuine warmth that I can't seem to fake and the common fucking sense his son can't fake. He shakes hands and shakes again. Nods and understanding. Blok dismisses me and I stand in the back, respectful and silent in my cheap suit. Young Jarrington is next to me for lack of anything better to do. His father introduces him around. You remember my son. Oh of course. Hands shake again but less warmly. Something not quite there in Young Jarrington. The dirty work more apparent in his face. The money. My introductions perfunctory. I'm not the heir apparent. I'm not old. No one has any doubts about where my hands have been. After the briefest pleasantries civility will allow, no one wants to talk to me. To Young Jarrington. We stand at the back of our chapel like we're the ones out of place. Soft hymns crackle through the speakers. It doesn't sound that bad in the pews but from back here it's obvious we'll need to replace the sound system soon. We pipe soft Brahms and Mozart through when children die. Twinkle twinkle and lullabies. It's one of the few things that still horrifies me here but it does seem to go over well with the families. They don't get "How I wonder what you are" stuck on repeat in their head when they reconstruct a fontanel. A guy I trained with in mortuary school said he packed soft heads with what was basically sawdust. I have never blamed the families for not wanting to talk to me. I open my pocket notebook and pretend to be writing. Pretending to be busy helps.

I excuse myself to get a drink of water and leave Young Jarrington to our sentry duty. As I emerge from the chapel I see the bereaved daughter in-law speaking softly with someone right in front of the water fountain, though, so I nod politely when she looks up and I keep on walking. To cover I duck into the men's room in the main hallway. There is an older man standing at the sinks, looking at himself in the mirror. He is a brother or an uncle or cousin of someone. He's family but not close. We were introduced but I don't remember his name. He doesn't acknowledge me, just keeps looking at himself. Slowly straightens his tie. Brushes nothing from his lapels. I enter a toilet stall and slowly close the door behind me. I don't want to sit my dress pants on the seat but I also don't want to stand here wiping down the seat with him standing at the mirror right outside the stall. Listening. I then worry about someone walking in and looking below the door for feet to see if the stall is occupied. If they do, they'll just see shoes and unlowered trousers. I will look like I'm just hiding. Which I am, by this point, but I don't want to look like I am. I lower my trousers around my ankles and wait for the man to leave. Get the fuck on with it. Your tie is straight. Think about your own mortality and have your breakdown somewhere else. When the man is gone I wipe instinctively, despite not actually using the toilet. Wash hands. Straighten tie. Brush lapels. I make quicker work of it.

People are still milling about, catching up and timidly approaching the casket when I re-enter the chapel. Old Jarrington catches my eye and with an eyebrow asks if we're ready to start. I nod once. Turn away to resume my post at the back. Out of the way. My stride breaks and a man behind me nearly walks into me as he moves to a seat. Athene is at the back of the church. Her head dipped towards Young Jarrington. He speaks to her and gestures minimally with his hands. After each gesture they return to the practiced easiness of a light clasp in front of him. Our respectful quiet stance, like a soldier at ease. Or no, wait. Do they keep their hands behind their back? Whatever. To see him like this it looks like he's guarding his dick. Athene smiles up at me as I approach.

"Oh, Ian. Glenn was just saying he thinks he knows where my mother is—what did you call it, Glenn?"

"Interred."

"Yes, right. He thinks he knows where my mother's remains are interred."

Son of a bitch. I doubt it.

"Yes, well. I remember because I knew your. The husband, you see. He was the butch. That is, he used to work at a deli I went to and so I—."

"Yes, well. It was a murder, the circumstances probably stick in the memory," Athene says. And she says it kind of shittily. But it bails Young Jarrington out so he nods somberly. Thin-lipped polite smile. I haven't said anything yet. I look at Jarrington.

I think your dad wants to start the flower procession.

"Very good," Young Jarrington says. Athene watches me. "I'll let them know outside."

Thanks.

The only nice thing about having arranged what is sure to be a catastrophic failure is that this is my show. When messages need to be run I can get Young Jarrington to run. I've got his daughter picking up last minute supplies for the private family viewing to follow the service. Getting the show put on is our ultimate authority, and when I'm running it I have some semblance of control. Except for the smile aimed up at my eyes.

Jesus Christ, Athene.

She's changed into a black pencil skirt and dark striped blouse. Dark stockings. Heels. She looks entirely appropriate. I want to fuck her eyes out.

"Ian?"

I turn and Becky is standing behind me. Looking at Athene. My mind spins fast. Does math. She can't possibly know. This can't even look bad. She's dressed right. She's a mourner. This is a funeral. Why is Becky even here? She's visited me at work all of three times, never in the chapel. Never anywhere beyond the front room, actually. Not that I blame her for that. Athene has been deeper into this world than she has. Becky is looking at her, though. Staring. Something about the way we're standing? She can smell something. No I'm paranoid. Why? A pre-recorded organ begins to grind its heavy doldrums into the room. The chapel doors open and the first of the rose-carrying children emerge. I resume my attentive, respectful pose and try to disappear into the wall like I'm supposed to. Guard my dick. Athene copies my posture on one side. Becky gawks at us. I gesture to her to move towards us. Stand on my other side. She crosses in front of me and stands next to Athene instead. More family with roses enter and move towards the former Mr. Bellanov. The children indelicately stab their flowers into the vase before the casket. I risk a small turn of my head and see Becky's head bow towards Athene. Becky is wearing sweatpants. One of my hoodies. Young Jarrington enters behind the next wave of the procession. Grandnieces and nephews now. Young Jarrington glides to the wall and assumes his sombre stance on the other side of Becky. Doesn't even look at her.

Sometimes this happens. The priest starts talking or the ceremony starts and people get caught out of their seat. No one knows. It's fine. No one even looks at Becky. At Athene. At Me.

YOU

We set things up to fail by over-complicating them. You are spectacular at this. Your plan is that a flower vase at the front of the chapel will receive roses as you and your family walk in. You propose three levels of family members, each with a different rose colour assigned. Red for immediate family. Yellow for close friends. White for extended family and other. The rest of the family in the planning room falls in behind you.

All we can do is gently explain that this might be a bad idea. When there are four or so people with you in a planning session we can usually steer you clear of most stupidity. But you have brought eight with you today. The inner circle of the family, with you at the head. Now, with that many in the room we are quickly ganged up on. Because someone too-quickly agrees with you that it would be lovely. Then their spouse agrees and all of a sudden it's decided. You have already bought the roses. This is happening. You decide that you don't need to tell people why they have been assigned which colour, it's enough that *you* know. It gets better. You won't just have the red ones go first, followed by yellow, then white. No, you decide to stagger them. Red, yellow, white, as people walk in. For the effect, one of them says, backing you up. But there are more whites than red and yellow due to the way families get larger the wider out the relation spirals, so after the first few waves it will have to switch to red, yellow, white x2. Then everyone will have to reorganize (meaning we will have to organize them in the melee) to sit with their respective families because when lined up according to rose colour they are fragmented by family grouping. This will not do.

Now there is not infinite room at the front of a church. What we will witness is the vase becoming stuffed halfway through so people will be shoving their roses into it. This plus a crush of people that can't sit down due to having to reorganize to sit as family units plus an old and sometimes uneven floor equals our expectation that the vase will fall over at some point during the procession. Perhaps it will shatter. It, too, is old.

We suggested multiple vases to you but this was met with stark horror. It *needs* to be one vase. You have to be *unified* as a family. The commitment to the metaphor is off-putting and we do not point out that the very act of stratifying the rose colours seems to fly in the face of your project. We would argue, but our job requires us to be somewhat sycophantic. And by somewhat, we mean we are sycophants. You would not tolerate us otherwise. There is no way to explain to you that this will absolutely not succeed without a rehearsal without you becoming enraged. We can make suggestions, but we are not to tell you how your grief works. We actually know how your grief works. Our business model is based upon it. But this is not what we will say. We are sycophants. We will sigh and go along with it and know that a funeral is not a wedding. You can't do showy things and expect them to work. Or, *you* can. You will. But you shouldn't. You will blame us if the vase breaks. We should have done a better job of organizing the aisles, you will say. Of making sure people reorganized quickly. You will not question why there needed to be a rose procession in the first place. This, we understand, is not in your nature.

You will have your show. You will wield your red rose and pause before the dead. We do good work, you will acknowledge that. You will grumble at the cost of our quality, but you will recognize it. You will not step aside quickly and a logjam will develop even more quickly than we expected. Well. You will look around for us. See us approaching in our measured, respectful shuffle. You will remember people are looking at you. Those behind you in the procession and those not involved in the procession, those who didn't even merit an "other" white rose, are watching. You will wipe any trace of annoyance off your face and replace it with the serene calm of control. The sombre piety of intelligent mourning. No keening here. You are in control. You will smile at some faces you recognize. You will perhaps notice faces you do not recognize. You will recognize among us a young man coming forward to help with the chaos. You will perhaps think he was not quite as respectful as he should have been, being one of us as he is. You will remember he is not family and perhaps you will be annoyed at having been assigned to what you perceive as an understudy. You will not recognize the young woman and the younger woman he was standing with. You will likely not notice if one of them is wearing sweat pants. We are trying to organize things now and you have other things on your mind. Possibly grief, but certainly annoyance with us. You will not make note of whether the women speak to one another or not. You will not read their faces or gestures. You will not recognize a need or story there. We feel this is for the best; you have your own needs. You are creating your own story with roses and drapes and the harshest grade in the industry fluids that were used because of the advanced rate of decay. You took your time planning. This story, you feel, must be told. You will know with certainty that it must be told. We will meet your eyes as the vase falls. We will watch you watch us as we and you and they wait to see if it will shatter.

Jon R. Flieger's work has appeared in *Canadian Literature, CV2,* and *The Malahat Review.* He was the winner of the 2011 Norma Epstein national award for fiction. His book *Never Sleep with Anyone from Windsor* (Black Moss, 2007) won the Orison award. He resides in Windsor, Ontario.